MW01493966

Saneatsu Mushanokōji

THE INNOCENT

Translated from the Japanese by
Michael Guest

Furin Chime
Sydney

This is a Furin Chime book, Sydney, Australia
furinchime.com

Originally published as Saneatsu Mushanokōji's *Omedetaki Hito* by the imprint
Rakuyōdō (Shirakaba), Tokyo, in 1911 (Meiji 44).

The Innocent is a translation derived from the Japanese text. A facsimile of the
Rakuyōdō edition is available from the National Diet Library Digital
Collections, Tokyo, Japan.

This translation aims to foster public appreciation and understanding of this
important historical piece of Japanese literature. By conveying its artistic and
cultural significance, we hope to contribute to its cross-cultural appreciation.

We are grateful to the estate of Saneatsu Mushanokōji for granting
permission for this translation to be published and
distributed globally.

ISBN 978-0-6487517-5-5

To Dr. Heizaburo Takashima

With a thousand thanks
I dedicate this little book to you

I believe in a selfish kind of literature, a literature for its own sake. It is only in accord with this idea that I desire to be an author. The value of my writing is determined by the degree to which it can harmonize with the reader's own individuality. I am not entitled to demand that people unable to empathize with me should buy or read what I write. The cover image [of the original edition] was kindly provided by my friend Arishima Ikuma, whom I heartily thank. The frontispiece is the opening plate from Max Klinger's collection of etchings, *Intermezzi*.

~ Author

| Translator's Preface

Over a period of 265 years, the Tokugawa shogunate had enforced the isolation of Japan from the rest of the world, under its *sakoku* ("locked country") policy. By opening the country to a myriad of Western influences, the Meiji Restoration unleashed a tumultuous maelstrom of intertwined intellectual, aesthetic, and social ideas. In contention was the seed of an emerging "modern self."[1] The official aim of promoting individualism, which had been suppressed during the feudal reign of the Tokugawa shogunate, was politically intentional, in order to advance the nation's competitiveness in the modern world. It played out dynamically in the spheres of art and literature, reflected and informed in endeavors to assimilate and challenge Western traditional and naturalistic forms.

Saneatsu Mushanokōji (also known as Mushakōji) (1885–1976) was among the first writers, along with Katai Tayama, author of the novel *Futon* (1907), to explore the interplay of these forces within a personal sphere of self-analysis. Mushanokōji's 1910 novella *The Innocent* (*Omede-taki Hito*) is considered by some to have been the first true "I-novel," which is an uncompromising confessional form embedded in autobiography.[2] Note that while the form of autobiography is essential to the I-novel, there are also departures from it. *The Innocent* is indeed centered on the adolescent obsession that Mushanokōji had for his third love, a woman named Taka Hidaka.[3] However, the appearance of the author's father in the narrative is a factual anomaly: Viscount Saneyo Mushanokōji died when Saneatsu was two years old.

Mushanokōji was instrumental in founding the "White Birch" society, or Shirakabaha, a progressive and influential literary coterie, with students of the élite Gakushūin (Peers' School) in Tokyo, who were largely devoted to expressing and cultivating the self. Of these aristocrats, none was from a more illustrious family than Mushanokōji. In 1910 the group founded the literary and art magazine *Shirakaba*, in which Mushanokōji published some of his early writings.

Mushanokōji was so ideologically committed to his ideals of self-cultivation that in 1918 he founded a utopian village based upon them, Atarashiki-mura, or "new village," which still exists in Moroyama, Saitama Prefecture, its original location in Hyūga, Miyazaki Prefecture, having been flooded by the construction of a dam in 1939.[4] In China, Mushanokōji's social project attracted the attention of none other than a youthful Mao Zedong—as different as his ideas on individualism proved to be.[5]

The I-novel, this singularly significant genre in modern Japanese literature, "the most salient and unique form of Japanese literature,"[6] embodies a quest for an authentic expression of the self, "no matter what pain or embarrassment baring the truth might cause."[7] *The Innocent* is entirely governed by a perpetual and resolute drive towards confession and self-analysis. It is, moreover, on account of Mushanokōji's revolutionary use of a "colloquial" style that the distinguished novelist Kōji Uno acclaimed him as "founder" of the genre. [8]

Why then, one might wonder, has a work of such considerable importance and unique charm as *The Innocent* resisted translation into English? Is it, as Suzuki suggests, that Western critical interest in the self has declined since the 1960s, with the structuralist critique of the self-subject as an a priori entity; or that the modern Western literary consciousness is predisposed to fiction, rather than to the value placed by Japanese tradition upon an unmediated reality, upon "immediate lived experience"?[9]

I would argue that the idea of the self as an intellectually contested site is absolutely intrinsic to an apparent and at times bizarre dynamic in Mushanokōji's *The Innocent*. An idealistic and prudish young man, who admits to being "hungry for a woman," falls in love with an idealized girl, Tsuru, whose name means "crane," a hallowed symbol of longevity, luck, and fidelity. He obsesses over her, has a go-between propose marriage to her repeatedly, spies on her outside her school, but never once even speaks to her. It is not surprising that young Japanese readers sometimes misperceive the work as some sort of "stalker novel." A more sophisticated contemporary reader will discern a centrifugal force at play within the narrative, continually pushing away objective, naturalistic reality from the internal domain of the self, while simultaneously delving deeper inward. The story spirals ever closer to an obsessive solipsistic state, so much so that in a supplementary narrative or addendum, characters are reduced to imaginary beings within the mind of the protagonist, in a motion of negation surprisingly anticipatory of Samuel Beckett. This comparison is further pronounced by the author's metaphysical theme and dramatic format of the closing chapters. In his depiction of unconsciously resonating characters in the story of "Two People"—a sibylline personification of "spooky action at a distance"—Mushanokōji intriguingly foreshadows the playful modernism of Italo Calvino's *Cosmicomics* (1968). In the amusing existential sketch "What if Never Born," the character Toyō Nakata is a tantalizing ringer for Calvino's Mr. Palomar (1983).

It seems that there has existed something of an ethnocentrism affecting the perspectives of Western critics, who have to a great extent mistakenly relegated their interest in *The Innocent* to its literary historical value. Indeed, the novel concretely embodies a quest for individuality, as was experienced as a socio-psychological phenomenon during the era. But critics rarely mention the novella's clear elements of self-satire and innovative form, including what I have called its "centrifugal" motion: its eddying into a paradoxical state of solipsism and self-negation. Mushanokōji's avant-garde tones ring out clearly from the close of the Meiji period, to us in our post-modern era, to an extraordinarily personal, sensitive, and sincere effect.

Until the present, there has been no English translation of the work in its entirety, but only scholarly references to the Japanese original. The Japanese title *Omedetaki Hito* incorporates diverse meanings denoting a type of personality recognizable in Japanese, ranging from "special," "happy," and "auspicious," through "good-natured," "gullible," "foolish," and "fatuous," etc. Critics have attributed titles such as *A Blessed Person*, *A Naive Person*, *A Dim-witted Man*, *The Good-natured Soul*, and *Happily in the Dark*. The most usual, perhaps quasi-official title, since we find this translation at Japan's National Diet Library, as well as in the *Encyclopedia Britannica*, is "The Good-Natured Person," which lacks any meaningful connotation in English, and performs more a function of bibliographical reference rather than serving as an evocative title. I much prefer the eminent Donald Keene's use of *An Innocent* but with the definite article, which tends to reflect the novel's focus on character.[10] The expression projects a highly apposite ironic overtone, in light of the novella's subtly self-satirical vein. It allows for an ambiguous attribution, either to the narrator or to the idealized Tsuru. Furthermore, the suggestion of naivety attached to the word "innocent" consciously references an attack on the author made by a noted critic of the time, Chōkō Ikuta (1882– 1936), who had accused Mushanokōji of being too naively innocent (*omedetai*) to properly represent modern life.[11] This appears to be the very criticism discussed in the final chapter of *The Innocent*.

This edition features the basic format and frontispiece from the 1911 Rakuyōdō edition of the book, though it lacks the cover illustration that the author refers to in his dedication. The cover of our present translation features a photograph by the Austrian photographer Baron Raimund von Stillfried of a young woman in kimono (ca. 1870).

The frontispiece is the German Symbolist Max Klinger's etching *Bear and Elf* (1881), with its intriguing

Darwinist resonance. Mushanokōji's dedication is to the educator Heizaburō Takashima (1865–1946), the author's teacher at the Peers' School.

The illustration in Chapter 10, Hugo Höppener's *Zur Brautinsel* ("Bridal Island," 1893), does not appear in the Rakuyōdō edition, but having traced Mushanokōji's references, I considered it a most useful enhancement to the section of the text that describes and interprets the very sketch.

Mushankōji gives no proper name to the narrator, but uses a Japanese word for "oneself, myself, I, me": *jibun*. In the footnotes, I maintain the standard critical practice of using "Jibun" when referring to the first-person narrator of *The Innocent*.

Michael Guest   2023

TRANSLATOR'S PREFACE

Notes

1. Seiji M. Lippit, *Topographies of Japanese Modernism* (NY: Columbia UP, 2002), 7.
2. Tomi Suzuki, *Narrating the Self: Fictions of Japanese Modernity* (Stanford, Calif.: Stanford UP, 1996), 48.
3. Yoshihiro Mochizuki, *Rediscovering Musha-ism: The Theory of Happiness in the Early Works of Mushanokōji Saneatsu, (M.A. thesis, University of Hawai'i, 2005)*, 100, n.96.
4. Angela Yiu, "Atarashikimura: The Intellectual and Literary Contexts of a Taishō Utopian Village," *Japan Review*, 2008, 20: 203–230.
5. Yang Jisheng, *Tombstone: The Great Chinese Famine, 1958–1962* (London: Macmillan, 2012), 170.
6. Suzuki, *Narrating the Self*, 1.
7. Donald Keene, *Dawn to the West: Japanese Literature of the Modern Era* (NY: Holt, Rinehart, and Winston, 1984), 246.
8. Kōji Uno, "My personal view of the I-novel" (1925), qtd. in Seiji M. Lippit, *Topographies of Japanese modernism* (NY: Columbia UP, 2002), 29. The difference between the classical Japanese, which had been the written standard, was so great that many people were unable to understand it. Mushanokōji was a pioneer in his use of the vernacular.
9. Suzuki, *Narrating the Self*, 3-4.
10. Keene, *Dawn to the West*, passim.
11. Keene, *Dawn to the West*, 450.

The Innocent

1

On the morning of January 29, I went to Maruzen bookshop to look for some books and left after buying one titled *Civilization and Education*, written by someone named Münch. When I came to the fourth corner along the street, I wondered if I should turn right or go straight ahead, and looked to my right for a moment. Two young women in flowery kimonos were standing a couple of dozen yards away, seemingly waiting for someone. My feet turned in their direction. I assumed the women were geisha. When I see a woman in a flowery kimono, with a round face, heavily powdered, I naturally think of her as a geisha.

Neither of them was beautiful, but they were not ugly either. One in particular had a certain charm about her.

Passing by them, I gave a casual look, saying to myself, "I hunger for a woman."

In fact, I was starving for one. Unfortunately, I crave a beautiful young woman. I have not even spoken to one since Tsukiko, my crush when I was nineteen, returned to her hometown seven years ago, and now I hunger for a woman.

Walking quickly I reached the moat and, instead of catching an electric tram, turned left to follow the tracks to Hibiya and go through Hibiya Park to my house.[1]

Passing through Hibiya, I saw a young couple talking cheerily. More than rejoicing in their happiness, I envied them for it, and cursed them even more than I envied. I wondered whether my feelings were the same as those a poor person has towards a rich one. I was immersed in my own solitariness, and the couple reflected my desolation straight back at me. It was acutely painful, the wound of my lost love. So instead of celebrating them in their joy, when they pierced me so acutely, I could not help but curse them instead.

How I hunger for a woman.

I went back to my house thinking of Tsuru.

Tsuru was a delightful and beautiful girl who lived near my home, but I had never spoken to her. I knew her from the time Tsukiko was still in Tokyo, so of course I did not love her at that time, but I thought she was a lovely child. I longed to be with her, and whenever I saw her, the thought of her lingered for a time afterward. In the third year after Tsukiko's return to her hometown, though, the bitterness of my lost love faded. Tsuru grew increasingly lovely and adorable, and I missed her if I hadn't seen her for a while.

At that point, I began to desire her. I came to think that there was no one more suitable to be my wife than her. It seemed to me that we could marry without compromising my individuality. She came to appear in my eyes as the ideal wife for whom I longed.

I had a craving for a woman, and Tsuru became the

object, such that I began to love her more and more. I came to feel it would be a blessing if she became my wife.

When I decided to marry her, my first worry was that people around me would ridicule and use me as a topic for gossip. Every time I went out for a walk, I would be pointed at and mocked.

I told myself it would be foolish to abandon my own and Tsuru's happiness because of such a consideration. That would be a spineless attitude indeed. I would need to show people that I was not afraid of them. Next door lived a rickshaw shop owner, whose wife was an inveterate gossip. I was going to have to withstand the backbiting, name-calling, and ridicule of the slack-jawed calligrapher, the greengrocer, and the local brats.

A further worry was my mother, who was a person terrified of everything. Having her neighbors laughing at her would be unbearable for her. However, she loved me and would surely stand by me, whatever I decided.

If I could get my mother on my side, my father, who found the whole world idiotic, would be certain to go along with her.[2]

Thus I determined to work as hard as I could to make Tsuru my wife. At the beginning of the following year, I obtained my mother's approval, and that spring, my father's. In the summer, it was decided to arrange for a go-between to make a proposal to her family.

Things were proceeding much more smoothly than anticipated, and seemed to be working out perfectly. During that period, I became quite confident and started to feel that my family household was actually superior to hers in many ways. I enjoyed happy, titillating dreams of things to come.

Our first meeting, sharing our mutual feelings, our first kiss . . . I fantasized about all such things, as well as imagining the rumors that would circulate among my friends and other people around me. I imagined how Tsuru would behave towards my father, mother, brother, sister, and niece. These fantasies were vivid and bright—but also somewhat shameful.

The go-between visited Tsuru's house in late July, but my proposal was brusquely rebuffed, with the words, "She is still young, and doesn't want to consider marriage for now." Thankfully my name was not mentioned, so when I next encountered her, remaining anonymous, I was able to see her face as clearly as before.

The same autumn, her family relocated from where they lived near my home to a place about a mile away. At the time, I had an inkling they may have moved because they were uncomfortable having learned that it was I who proposed. I was lonely, missing the few opportunities I had to catch sight of her. Until March of the following year, I went to see her once every month on her way home from school. Sometimes I went once a week, but was not bold enough to go any more often than that.

In March, the go-between, a man named Kawaji, went to Tsuru's family to propose for me again. This time he gave them my name. He conveyed to them how I loved her and would wait for as long as necessary to marry her. In actuality, I had such a hunger for a woman I could barely wait another day. Furthermore, I had heard that Tsuru would be graduating from school that spring.

But she did not graduate from school in the spring. I was told she did not want even to hear about it until her brother was married. After that, I ran into her once by chance on the Kōbu tram. That was April 4, which was the last time I saw her. . .

Tsuru's story has remained unchanged ever since. I wonder whether there is any hope for me.

That about encapsulates the relationship between myself and Tsuru.

I have yet to know a so-called woman.

Occasionally I see a naked woman in my dreams. That is not a genuine woman, though, but an androgynous one.

I am twenty-six years old this year.

I hunger for a woman.

I have no doubt that Tsuru is more than capable of satisfying my hunger. Therefore, I am still in love with her, even though I have not seen her for almost a year. Perhaps because I have not seen her, she has become increasingly close to my ideal woman.

So for now, I have no desire to marry another woman, no matter how many years go by until this story is concluded.

However, I am hungry for a woman. A beautiful young woman other than Tsuru would instantly attract me. Indeed, older women, even those who are not so beautiful, attract me with considerable force at certain moments.

Nature has created men and women to be drawn to each other. For this reason, I sometimes experience loneliness and pain, but I am grateful that nature created man and woman and for their strong attraction to each other. If there were no women on earth . . . If there were no one to love. If there were no one for whom to yearn. Only dead souls gathered together, absorbed in their self-interest. How lonely that would be.

There are some people who are corrupted by a woman. But how many are able to live with a woman? How many people know the value of being given birth by a woman? A woman herself may be boring. (Maybe as boring as a man, or even more so.) But there is something that exists between a man and a woman.

Indeed, women are considered "eternal idols" by men.

While Eve may have caused Adam to be expelled from the Garden of Eden, it was better for him to be expelled together with her rather than to have remained there alone.

I may not have known a woman, but I know the power that a woman has over a man. She may herself be powerless. But her power over a man is immense.

I wonder whether it is because I do not know an actual woman? I worship an ideal woman. I worship her flesh and her heart. Tsuru is the most ideal among all the women I know.

Magnificent Tsuru!

Yet, no matter how much I hunger for a woman, no matter how much I love Tsuru, I will not give up my work in order to obtain her. I love my own self more than I love her. No matter how lonely I am, I will not sacrifice myself to have her. I want to marry her even if I have to eat two meals a day instead of three, and even if I have to live in any sort of squalid old house. Still, I cannot think of sacrificing my ego to unite with her.

When I hungered for a woman, I came to know the power of women, and when I came to know the power of women, I learned the power of my own self.

The soft, rounded body of a woman. Her gentle heart. Her bewitching fragrance. Her heart that can soothe the heart of another. I want with all my soul to dance with a woman. How I need spring to arrive, before I lose all spirit.

Even for the sake of cultivating my own self do I desire Tsuru.

2

I arrived home a little before lunch.

Mother, myself, and my niece, who had turned four this year, lunched together. Father went to the office every day, and my older brother and his wife were overseas on company business.

My niece Haru-chan was spending the day with her grandmother. When my father returned, he had his own business to attend to, though he is devoted to his granddaughter.[1]

I love Haru-chan too. She calls me "uncle-chan" and is very fond of me, but I cannot say that I am totally enamored. I live at home without anyone to love but myself.

It was a cheerful meal with Haru-chan. I don't know how many times my mother and I laughed. The child is truly endearing, even when she is annoyed or being selfish and starts crying. But even when she laughs, I am not as enchanted with her as Mother is. Other people's children may be adorable, but my niece is much more so. One's own children are probably the most adorable of all.

I find Haru-chan cute, but I am preoccupied. Sometimes I feel faintly repulsed when Mother, or especially

Father, becomes quite so enthralled. Nevertheless, if I had children of my own I would be enthralled as well. My wife and I would both be in raptures together with them.

We finished our meal and I returned to my room.

I was fine during lunch, but back in my room I became lonely and started to miss Tsuru, whom I had not seen for a long time. Yet I felt uncomfortable about going to see her, which would only make me feel lonelier. I am sure she has no say in regard to our marriage.

Still, not knowing how she is, I do so much desire to see her.

Then I realized it was a Friday. I am a rather superstitious person and entertain a belief in fate, having no faith in human intelligence. While not believing strongly enough to rely on fate, I accept it to some degree. You might say I am relatively superstitious. I believe in fate even as I dismiss it. At the very least, I do pay it some heed.

I have heard that Fridays are considered unlucky by Westerners. For two or three years now, I have resisted going out to see her on Fridays, even when I wanted to. Still, sometimes I venture out, albeit unwillingly, because such superstitions are misguided. Since she moved house, I had to go further to see her. Even though I especially didn't want to go on a Friday, I would sometimes go anyway, knowing it would be superstitious not to. It would be better if I did not see her when I was like that.

I had not seen Tsuru in almost a year but found the prospect of going out on a Friday disagreeable. Yet I wanted to see her.

I decided that for such a precious, long-awaited meeting, it made little difference whether the circumstances were favorable or unfavorable and it might be best not to see her at all. Thus I abandoned the idea.

Happily!

I picked up Münch's book but could not bring myself to read it. I was lonely and couldn't help feeling that I was merely an imaginary person, unable to do or say anything worthwhile. At times I have a premonition I am going to die young from a natural disaster. Probably just a fantasy, but I am sure I will be killed by a lightning strike or a meteorite.

Alternatively, I might die young from lung disease. Somehow I fancy that I will not live long, but will immediately feel as if I can live forever and do not believe I will die any time soon. Then again, natural disasters can be lethal, especially lightning and meteorites.

Great talents mature late. I am a man of the future, one of high degree, but when the time comes, I must die, no matter how hard I resist. I wish I were someone who had nothing to achieve, but I have many things to do and would hate to die.

In any case, I have not been able to taste love, nor do any work I enjoy. I do not know the joy of being a father and cannot help feeling as if I am going to die.

I went outside to dispel my loneliness.

The day was gloomy and overcast. In the same mood, I walked aimlessly through the colorless town, a solitary feeling in my heart. I was unable to cry, but as I walked my loneliness worsened and I became tearful. I felt as if my personality had risen to a superior level. I felt as if I were better than the other people in the street. I felt pity and sympathy for everyone.

What is the purpose of your life? I asked myself, in the depth of my heart.

Are you living for your country, your home, your parents, your husband, your children, or yourself?

Is it for the sake of the one you love? Do you have anyone to love?

3

The next day, the 30th, was a Saturday. An alumni meeting was arranged at a friend's house in Ōkubo. It had been raining lightly until noon, but by the time I left home at about one o'clock in the afternoon to go to Ōkubo, the showers had lifted so much that I hardly needed an umbrella. I walked to Yotsuya, furling and unfurling my umbrella along the way, and took the Kōbu tram.[1]

Tsuru lived in Ōkubo! I didn't know exactly where, but it turns out to have been about a hundred doors away from my friend's house.

I seldom visited my friend, but the times I went there after Tsuru moved house, I could not help thinking of her, and wondering if we might be traveling together on the tram.

Perhaps we might meet along the way.

I had to wait quite a while to get on the tram, but there was no one who looked like Tsuru. I alighted at Ōkubo and was surprised at how bad the street was along my way. The surface was so uneven at one point, that one of the teeth on my high *geta* clogs was nearly knocked off, which goes to show just how shocking the streets are in that part of town.[2]

It occurred to me that Tsuru had to go along this awful road every day on her way to school. I was reminded of a time a year before last, when I had visited her.

"Run and see!" I smiled, mouthing the words to myself.

It was the year before last, when, wanting to see her, I went out to her school. Not wishing to go straight up to the entrance, I stayed on the main street for some distance further, heading for the next right turn. As I approached it, I could not see any sign of her. When I had come about thirty meters, I saw a group of four or so female students standing at the corner, looking around behind them.

Someone was running after them, doing their best to catch up.

I wondered if it were Tsuru. Not an unusual thought. Whenever I see a female student of her age, or a woman coming from a distance, or a woman from behind, whatever the time or place, I wonder whether it might be Tsuru. I can notice this tendency increasing, little by little. Ten times out of ten it would not be her.

And yet still I wonder.

This time, though, it was Tsuru who came running up, wearing high *geta*, running madly after them. The weather was fine that day. So was the road. The girls waiting were all wearing low *koma-geta*.[3]

Her face flushed, she came running up to them and bowed, saying, "Thank you for waiting."

At this point, I would not have been fifteen feet away from her. Looking at her for a moment, I made to turn right. Then Tsuru said something. I heard the others answer, "Because you were running too fast!" At that moment, I was already rounding the corner. She was bending down to pick up the tooth that had come away from her high *geta*.

At that moment, I fancied that she and I exchanged glances. I walked on in a daze for another thirty meters. When I turned around, no one was there anymore.

I had the thought that Ōkubo was a place with bad roads. So that memory came flooding back again.

"Run and see!" would be something I would say to tease her, after we were married, when we put on our high *geta* to go out walking together. The time may never come when we can tease each other. Yet, in my imagination I can do it as much as I like.

When I arrived at my friend's house, there were already four or five people there.

Eventually more assembled, until there were about fifteen. Some I had not seen in three or four years. Among them were officers at military college. Others have gone on to become scholars.

Some have wives and children.

When we get together, everyone returns to a time six or seven years ago. We are all friends from then. Those who cannot inhabit the mindset from that past era cannot enthuse in each other's company at one of these events. Our age is a factor that does not affect the conversation.

One group of as many as five or six were eagerly discussing geisha. Among them were even some members who had in the past disdained talk of that sort. I had the thought that these fellows had become hungry for a woman too. It was disconcerting to see their brazen, idiotic interest in the conversation reflected on their faces. I was uncomfortable listening, but from time to time, could not help overhearing some offensive scraps. Somebody or other was loved by a geisha or had fallen in love with one. Someone uttered the words "department store," which popped into my ear.

Listening to their stories, I decided that I ought never to indulge in geisha, no matter how strongly I hunger for a woman. I do not envy men who enjoy a night with a beautiful woman in this way.

At the previous alumni meeting, it came out that so-and-so had taken a spouse. That became a topic again this year, along with talk about items such as who had become engaged to marry, who pre-engaged, and so on. Someone was talking sarcastically about someone else having become a father.

As a moral scholar, I find it unacceptable to make jokes about sexual issues like this, and to bandy around solemn matters merely for the sake of recreation.[4]

Hence my own ideas about women. I can't help but think that there is a huge discrepancy between the way different people think about marriage. Everything was fine when we were enjoying ourselves chatting, but when the gossip started, the words coming out of their mouths made me feel disinclined to come and see them again in future.

They are no doubt men who would giggle at the sight of Rodin's *The Kiss*.

Despite all that, by and large, today's reunion was a great success. Not a single person was as intoxicated as at previous alumni meetings, not one with even a hint of red in his face. One cannot allow oneself to become drunk with people like them, considering their interests.

It was after ten o'clock when everyone went home laughing out loud, chorusing about having eaten and exerted themselves too much, and they all said they'd enjoyed themselves. They had never experienced such childlike amusement anywhere else.

We traveled cheerfully together by tram as far as Yotsuya. There we split up to go our separate ways. It had stopped raining, but there was a haze around us and the sky was thick with clouds. The clouds had grown darker, grayish at the edges. They were moving fast, and the moon, on this the seventeenth day of its cycle, would sometimes show its bright face.

I mused while walking back through the quiet, gas-lit city streets.

If only I were able to marry Tsuru. . . If I attended an alumni meeting then, the same sneerers would probably be there. I would repay their ridicule with righteous indignation. No one ridicules me because to do so means to fight with me in the true sense of the word. They may feel free to mock as hard as they like, as far as I am concerned, but nobody dares.

Our marriage would make a good topic for gossip, and those fools might still try ridiculing me.

If they did, I would answer them like this:

"Yes, it was love at first sight and we married. I am sorry to say that I cannot be interested in as many women as you are because I know something of true love. I cannot do everything."

While I spoke, I would make an expression as though I

were biting through a bitter-tasting bug. It would be most awkward. Yet I am unable to rise above reacting like this.

If I am able to transcend that, I am already no longer a moral scholar. No longer an educator.

If everyone remained silent at that moment, I would probably just change the subject. But I knew that if someone wanted to ridicule me, I would be unable to hold my peace. I smiled at the thought.

I arrived home at around 11:30 and immediately settled into my cold bed.

4

On the evening of February 1, my friend Nakano came to see me.

This person knew of my present love. He was a classmate at school and now studies literature at university. He was at the alumni meeting on the 30th. We talked of various things, but the words that made an indelible impression were these:

"That beautiful girl who used to ride the tram to school seems to be acquiring something of a reputation, doesn't she?"

I said, "Yes, I suppose so. We all hunger after a beautiful woman, don't we?"

Tsuru must have a reputation as well! I believe she commuted to school by tram from Ōkubo.

My friend talked about what he had heard from people, concerning two or three women with reputations.

I did not know these women, so I thought nothing of their reputations. I definitely did not want Tsuru to gain one. How repugnant for her name to be on the lips of those who think of a woman as a plaything. Tsuru is not flamboyant in any way. She wears a plain kimono quite carelessly (at least until last year) and does not stand out. She is beautiful, though. Beautiful in whichever the style. Such a lovely, gentle appearance. She possesses qualities attractive to men. The face of Mary. Eyes like Venus.

It is impossible for this woman to escape the eyes of a hungry man.

She would have a reputation by now.

I feel as if something sacred has been defiled.

I wish I were the only one entitled to love her. For some reason, for the past five years I have entertained a superstition that Tsuru's individual characteristics can be wedded to mine alone. Even though we have never spoken, I believe nature has given me the power to embrace her utterly.

Possibly there is no one else who loves her. All the same, I am not so naive as to think so.

Suppose there is someone who does love her. I would be curious about his character. If he is sincere in his love, then my future happiness will cause him misery. And for Tsuru to give her heart to him but have to come to me at her parents' behest would be heartbreaking for her. I could not then marry her in good faith.

I have no wish to make someone unhappy for the sake of my own pleasure, nor to make someone sacrifice their love in my interest. How could I be pleased by the misfortune of the woman I loved? It was because I believed it would be in Tsuru's best interest to be with me, and because I thought she loved me, that I went to great lengths to seek my parents' reluctant consent to my intention to propose. But if Tsuru was unhappy about coming to me and wanted to marry someone else — someone more promising, respectable, and good-looking — then I would need to reconsider.

How terrible it would be for her to come to me feeling she would be happier somewhere else!

If she were to accept my proposal joylessly, then I would have to withdraw it. By nature, I am a moralist.

And as such, an extreme individualist.

I am against sacrificing myself in the slightest for the sake of another person and would be ashamed to sacrifice another in my own interest.

Moreover, the thought of constraining someone's freedom and will because of my love for them is anathema to me. My beloved should not be unhappy for my benefit.

At the same time, I had no idea whether Tsuru loved somebody else. I doubted whether she was in love with me, but was sure there was no one else.

I am egotistical enough to doubt there could be anyone of better character who loves her than I.

Here the problem is turned around. She might marry somebody better looking than me, simply because I have not pressed her hard enough. She might die without knowing the joy and gratification of life with me.

The thought occurred that the time had come for me to fight for Tsuru.

I have not seen her for almost a year. I have never spoken to her. Nonetheless, I believe that during the past three to four years, our hearts have not been strangers. It is a selfish belief, but I have held such thoughts for some years now, ever since I began seriously reading Maeterlinck.[1]

You can lie with your mouth or with your ears, but a

sincere heart does not lie. This I believe. Not so much, though, to leave no room for doubt.

I said this to myself while conversing with Nakano.

I was detached and thinking it in silence.

After Nakano left at nearly eleven, saying he would miss his tram, I was moved by a strong feeling of compassion, and resolved to do my utmost to make Tsuru and myself a couple. I wrote a letter to Mr. Kawaji, my go-between.

Even writing the preface, I saw how arrogant I was being towards Tsuru.

Hungry for a woman, I had reasoned that if we could not become a married couple directly, we could at least get engaged. And now I realized she was still only eighteen. I had thought she already turned eighteen three or four years ago. She has an older brother, but she is an only daughter. Her parents must have felt uneasy about letting their lovely girl leave them at such a young age to spend her life in the hands of a man whose nature was unknown to them. These days many people marry in their twenties and thirties. The majority. Presumptuously, I consider myself a good person, but Tsuru's parents and brother—he knew me—must have thought I was an undisciplined, lackadaisical individual. An unpleasant, undesirable man, purely infatuated with women. Somebody without hope or promise. It was entirely natural they think that.

All I have going for me is that my father has a level of reputation, my older brother good prospects, and I do not have to worry about food.

Unless there is no alternative, they will not give me a second thought. In a couple of years they will not even mention me. In the meantime, they will be certain to take advantage of any opportunity that comes up. Beyond doubt, someone more qualified will fall in love at the sight of her and propose.

Even if she does love me, she could never bring herself to disobey her parents and brother's wishes.

The thought made me forlorn. I wrote the following in my letter to Mr. Kawaji:

. . . I have loved and yearned for love selfishly. Because of this, I have caused trouble for many people. I regret the nuisance I have been to you, who are a particularly busy man.

It is a godsend that matters have come so far. I am blessed that a suit such as mine has been able to progress to this stage without being misunderstood.

Therefore, even if my proposal is in vain, I am forever grateful to all those who understood, sympathized, and worked so hard trying to bring it to fruition. In token of my appreciation, I will not lose heart in the slightest if on this occasion I am unsuccessful, but will continue to move forward in my own direction.

Please believe in me. Your belief in me is my strength.

I still have my original intention regarding the issue. I will never give up. While a glimmer of hope remains, I will not despair and abandon my wishes. So I need to bother you once again.

I wish to adjust my course. I beg you to go a further time to the other party, since I am willing to wait until the time comes when marriage can be discussed. Please notify me when that occasion arises. Furthermore, although it must be troublesome for you, I kindly request that you inform me as soon as you can if an alternative suitor is accepted.

Please do me the immense service of conveying these matters.

It is foolish to propose marriage over and again when the other wishes to decline. If the other person wants not to progress, not to be with me, I cannot think they would wish me to continue to bow my head and propose.

It is not right to make someone unhappy, with my selfish desire to give and receive love.

I pray for the joy of my beloved. I do not wish for my beloved to be unhappy.

I had decided even before her parents refused consent that I would remain single until she married another. I am ready to wait for any number of years.

This is far from a matter of indifference to me, yet I will accept the need to assume an indifferent attitude as punishment for my selfish love.

Please bear with me and trust in the sincerity of my intentions. Have no reservations in contacting me. I am eternally indebted and remain your humble servant. Should the other party become someone else's wife, I kindly ask that you request her to notify me.

I am fully aware of the burdensome nature of my selfish requests and am truly sorry to trouble you with them, but it will make me terribly anxious if you are somehow unable to communicate these requests and settle matters urgently.

If you fulfill my request, I can leave matters to fate and follow my own path with some peace of mind. I continue to ramble long-windedly in my selfishness.

Forgive me.

I finished writing and when I looked at the clock it was a little before two. I went to bed before much longer. Being agitated, I found it impossible to sleep, and shed a tear for myself.

I am a man! A brave warrior! I have important work to accomplish. Tomorrow, I will become astonishingly diligent, I encouraged myself. I fell asleep in the middle of the night.

5

The next morning, I woke up around seven o'clock. Before eating, I went out to post my letter of the previous night. While doing so, I prayed for good fortune.

I am not very big on praying. But when I do, I feel somewhat safer. When I am worried or wish for something, I have a habit of praying with all my heart for a while.

Today the weather was fine for the first time in ages, with an invigorating chill in the air. I decided to commence my studies without being preoccupied with Tsuru.

No matter how I try, I cannot help but think about her. Still, I am not going to allow my mind to be distracted. It would be foolish to waste so much time.

I had already done everything in my power. I must not imagine her becoming my wife. Nor allow any lingering regrets of the sort, if only it might have been.

Regardless, I still wondered how she might be doing. Immediately, I wished for everything to go well, once again anticipating the ridicule of my neighbors. (*Tsuru, a word to you: When the world says these sorts of things, it only makes two people love each other more and more.*)

Breakfast was served at 8:30. Haru-chan was energetic as ever. Children of three and four are physically fit
and always so happy and eager to be with those who love
them. I watched on in fascination, spontaneously smiling to myself and reflecting on how truly precious my
mother and father must find her.

But in fact, they were both smiling and laughing with
slightly awkward expressions.

Just then I had a desire to see Tsuru's happy face. I
immediately gave up the idea, but could no longer smile.
I ate hurriedly, regarding my parents askance when they
became absorbed in their laughter, and giving just a little
smile when they tried to include me. I finished eating and
returned to my room, feeling alone and lonely.

I opened Münch's book and started reading, but could
not settle down.[1]

I wish to become an educator in the broadest sense; to
erect a new hall of knowledge in the place of a crumbling
one. I want to teach seekers of knowledge what it is they
curse in their heads but desire in their hearts.

I labor constantly under this burden, but I am weak. A
man without talent.

I am like ivy that creeps along the ground, longing for
the heavens but helpless. Grasping onto anything I en-
counter, I think, Ah, here is something with which to lift
myself up. In this respect, I am an optimist. First and
foremost, I wish to rely on Tsuru, but that seems impossible.

There is something I do not want to say at this point,
but feel it is necessary. I need to confess something that
nature has commanded me to keep secret. It concerns

the issue of lust. Nature has an awesome power to make us feel ashamed of the lustful cravings we all have. Think of how incoherent the relationship between men and women would be without shame! It is by using embarrassment that nature commands us to keep the subject as secret as possible. But I must respectfully disobey.

While unmarried, when tempted by lasciviousness, I try to escape by self-stimulation. Yet some people manage to live a good life without either masturbating or knowing a woman. Such a life would seem to be possible, given the power of human will and the faculty of reason. In spite of that, after a rather strong struggle, I have come to believe it is acceptable to masturbate. When a friend told me that Metchnikoff held the same opinion, it strengthened my conviction.[2] Even so, it seems a shameful thing, almost singularly shameful. Whenever my thoughts turn to such things, a voice in my mind says, "You are nothing but a vile masturbator." Perhaps one reason why I wanted to marry Tsuru as soon as possible was to rid myself of this source of shame.

Unable to sit still with Münch's book, I decided to go for a walk to Kanda. On the way, I met a friend from Koishikawa. He said he had been thinking of coming to see me, so we went back to my home together.

He was the oldest friend I had and I was very fond of him. He had graduated from a commercial high school three years earlier and was working at Mitsui. He is a pragmatic man who disdains daydreaming and fantasy. He dismisses moral principles as well, believing there is no virtue worth a damn. Virtue, he says, is the creation of the strong and the burden of the weak, and he equates the weak with the sick. Just as the sick suffer without being morally judged, neither should the weak be judged. There is no sense in feeling sympathy for either.

We frequently argue, but then we can exchange just a few words to put the dispute completely behind us.

In a word, we do not share the same ideology or interests but are in harmony in other respects.

On that day, we were talking about one thing and another, and found ourselves in a discussion about libertinism.[3]

"I am surprised that you still think of it as a bad thing. You cannot open your eyes," my friend remarked scornfully.

"I feel sorry for debauchers."

"You probably envy them."

"That may be so, but I also pity them. It is not unreasonable for a man who is starved for a woman to go out and pay for a prostitute or geisha as a means of solace and pleasure. But it is not a good idea. First of all, it is unnatural for women to be manipulated for money. It demeans them and negates the need for male-female relationships. A man's interest in a woman becomes vile, which may be convenient for the libertine, but must be unbearable for the woman."

"You speak from the female perspective, as one would expect from a prude," he said. "But a healthy man has rights as well. Someone who takes pleasure in life is entitled to do so, without having to go around like some kind of sexual invalid. You, as a scholar, should not derive satisfaction from the plight of the weak. I will not accept the idea that healthy people should be condemned for com-

plying with the demands of nature and enjoying themselves."

"Is it nature that drives them to debauchery? I am surprised that you are unaware of the damage it can cause."

"I have heard that nonsense, dammit, but there is no
harm in lust! The world does not work the way moralists
would like. It is not uncommon for a playboy to thrive
and a prude to be neurologically weak. Of course, a playboy may suffer consequences, depending on the situation. But those who denounce him for his debauchery
wish secretly they could have done the same. You prudes
should die peacefully, knowing it was your dedication to
your work that killed you."

"I am not talking about the visible harms of debauchery," I said, "but about the waste of energy, time, and
money that could be put to better use. The neglect of hob-
bies and interests. The playboy's craving when he is not
experiencing pleasure. The anxiety of perpetually yearning for a geisha. The destruction of peace in the home."

"Oh come now! A playboy has a sweet time simply
debauching. He can drink, fool around with women, and
do whatever he wants. They don't deal with individuals
but with pleasure per se."

"You would probably become crazed with all that lust."

"You may get carried away at times, but that is not a
problem. All you have to do is get as much pleasure out of
it as you can. Simply take pleasure in the moment, enjoy
that delightful feeling, and nothing is lost," he said.

"I would feel sorry for your wife."

"You would be just as well off not having a wife. Anyway,
if you manage things properly, you do not have to feel that

way. Women welcome a playboy more than a prig. First of all, strangely enough, they are bound to dislike a fellow like you, who is not the least bit shrewd. Women are foolish enough to think that a man who respects and loves them is effeminate. They consider a man inflexible and dull-witted who doesn't take his pleasures as he finds them. You have to be blunt about everything and be plain about what pleases you. Women believe what they hear. They lie a lot, but they are also easily deceived. The secret to getting a woman is first to occupy her body, and then her spirit will be inside of it. A man like you will never be loved by a woman. You can do no better than revolve around your beloved like the earth around the sun."

"You have gone completely off track." I was getting an earache, so I changed the subject.

My friend laughed incredulously and then said, "What happened about . . . that little matter?"

He knows about my love for Tsuru.

I told him about my friend's visit of the previous night and about my letter.

He did not laugh a bit. When I had finished my story, he said:

"Well, I hope it works out, and if it does, there will be no one happier than you. You are absolutely unqualified to be a playboy."

"I have no desire to be promiscuous," I said. "I am hungry for a woman, but long for the pleasure of just one woman."

'That's fair enough, I suppose, but it can't be all fun and games," my friend laughed.

'That may be so too, I'm afraid I must admit. But otherwise, if she were not there, perhaps I would have no pleasure whatsoever. That would be terrible. Maybe as bad as the time I have been having already."

We laughed and our discussion turned elsewhere.

He left before noon.

The next morning, on the third, Mr. Kawaji wrote back. "I understand your feelings entirely. I will consult with her father, and do everything in my power to accomplish a satisfactory result. I beg you to leave everything with me," the letter read.

Do your best!

May you be blessed with good fortune!

6

I lived my life as usual, striving eagerly to reach my goals, while continually wishing to be husband and wife with Tsuru.

The thirteenth of February was her birthday. I often forget my own birthday, June 11, but I have never forgotten Tsuru's since the time Kawaji-sensei told me about it at school. The thirteenth of February was a Saturday. I lunched at around 11:30 and, making out as though I had business, went out to see her. I felt somehow tight in my chest, happy, embarrassed, and worried.

How heart-warming to think that Dante must have felt something like this. Of course, it is a stretch to compare myself to Dante, even if I were to compare Tsuru to Beatrice. Anyhow, I am rather humble, so I may be able to marry Tsuru. I thought about this as I walked along.

I am an extremely lucky man and was therefore convinced that things with Tsuru would go well, at least for the time being. I was looking forward to seeing how she might feel, meeting me today, after not having seen me for a year. How strange it would be if she had forgotten about us having met.

Eventually, I reached a road where we should be able to bump into each other. I passed by a procession of students coming from her school. The road was not straight, but bent to the right about a hundred meters along. I could not see far beyond there. As I approached that point, no one resembling Tsuru was to be seen. She might appear at any second. I wondered how she would look. I walked on, paying close attention to the schoolgirls coming towards me. Now I could see some fifty meters ahead. If I kept going, Tsuru should come into view.

My heart pounded in my chest at the excitement of passing that point. Some twenty or so students were approaching, chatting together in groups of two or three. Perhaps Tsuru would be in the group of four at the end. Whenever I met her in the past, she was usually in a gathering of three or four.

But when they got closer, she was not among them. A disappointment, but a relief as well. An intermittent stream of girls came around the bend. As they chatted together, they walked in my direction, as though gravitating towards me.

However, their numbers gradually dwindled, and still Tsuru was not among them. Finally, I came to the bend, and at that point, the path split in two. If she appeared now, I would instantly turn right. No, I would take a glance to the left and turn right whether I saw her or not. To go left would be to pass by her school, and I was afraid to do that. Yet when I looked to the left, she was not to be seen, so I decided to turn left anyway.

I walked as slowly as I could. There were few girls coming from the gate anymore. Only three, and two of them went in the opposite direction. The one who came towards me did not remotely resemble Tsuru.

I soon passed by the school and took a quick look inside the yard. No one was there. It was deserted. Might she be ill? Even more worrying, perhaps she had changed her path because she did not want to see me. Even knowing that was impossible, I still had a feeling it was somehow true.

I chose the nearest road and headed back, feeling lonely, pitiful, and angry. If Tsuru became my wife, I was sure she would complain to me for not having met her in 1907, on her seventeenth birthday.

What would she say to me then?

When I got back home, I could not help feeling embarrassed and resentful. I went into my room and examined a painting by Ludwig von Hofmann to ease my feelings.[1] I looked for von Hofmann's book, but could not find it. Becoming more and more angry, I pressed hard on the bell.

Our live-in student came in response.[2]

"Did you not see a book like this, here on my desk?" I said, pointing at one from the same series, which lay there.

The young man said, "I don't know," and started searching, but could not find it. I was getting even angrier.

"There is nothing more aggravating than searching for books," I said. "From now on, don't touch any of my books." He said "Very well," and continued to search. There was no point in continuing to watch on, so I hauled out an armful of books from a shelf. He was in a panic that I was so furious. I seldom get angry at all. I started putting away books at random, and the one I was looking for appeared, just where I had left it.

I said, "There it is." He was relieved and went to put it away. I said, "You don't have to do that." As he was leaving, I said brusquely, "Thank you for your help."

When he left, I was irritated with myself for becoming angry at the innocent student. How short-tempered I had become those days.

It must, I thought, be because of my hunger for a woman. I was angry at my own low character. But my heart was still raging. I opened von Hofmann's book and looked at it, but even his wonderfully tranquil artworks could not comfort my heart. I closed the book and looked at some of Klinger's drawings. Then I turned to some by Greiner, which were so powerful they made my heart beat wildly. I strode through the room, summoning all my strength.[3]

Even if Tsuru does not become my wife, and I do not taste the tenderness of love, I will not allow my heart to be tormented. I must do all I can to transcend it.

Brave Warrior, Brave Warrior! I am a Brave Warrior!

I cried out in my heart, and in so doing, prevented something of an effeminate feeling from taking root there.

7

On the evening of February 15, I heard from my mother that my maternal uncle was suffering from cancer. My uncle, a good-natured person, was an unconventional man who enjoyed being stubborn, and he was a count in the Exalted Lineage of the Japanese Empire.[1] He and my father were close friends because they both enjoyed making fun of the world.

My uncle was an extraordinary eccentric. I still remember going to Miura-Misaki with my family for a summer vacation, and my uncle went strolling around in the nude. I was twelve years old and went with him one morning before breakfast to the master fisherman's house. He was stark naked, without even a *fundoshi*, and strode along as if he were unaware of being naked.[2] If he saw someone he knew, he greeted them as a matter of course. When we arrived at the master fisherman's, my uncle announced that he had come in his formal attire today, walked calmly into the room, and started conversing. Strange to think back now that I was also quite at ease accompanying him. He used to bathe in cold water, and when he went to the beach he would swim out into the ocean. He also drank a lot of alcohol. These things seemed very grand, during that era when I worshiped this eccentric man.

One day, my uncle went to Kōfu. It was before the steam train was in service, and he stayed at an inn along the way. He was unhappy with the way he was treated there, so he signed "*Shinheimin*"—"New Commoner"—in the register.[3]

He was welcomed in Kōfu by a viscount. When for some reason the police saw the derogatory name "New Commoner" written in the inn's register, they were astonished and reprimanded the innkeeper for his poor service. My uncle said he was sorry to hear that, and went back and stayed at the inn again.

He told me stories about his failed efforts to start up a company one time, and about how he was followed around by a detective after having had a love affair with a Chinese revolutionary.

I never knew him to suffer from any illness. He had a strong, lean body, and everyone took it for granted that he was at the peak of fitness. He partied and drank a lot. Three years earlier, a doctor warned my aunt that my uncle had the appearance of a man with alcohol poisoning and that he ought to be careful.

My uncle had still been walking around for a couple of months when his color changed dramatically and he started to lose weight. Understandably, he got worried and went to visit a doctor, who could not work out what was wrong. Both my aunt and uncle suspected he might have cancer. We also had our concerns, though no one ever voiced them publicly. The doctors did not believe it was cancer, since he was eating and defecating well. But his illness was evident. His pallor worsened, and even his ears lost their color. Everyone was secretly worried. My father and mother talked about how he might have been stricken with a deadly disease.

On February 6, he went to the Red Cross Hospital to be examined, but became too weak even to move and had to be hospitalized. After a blood and stool analysis, it was determined that he had cancer of the kidneys.

My mother said to my father, "When you have cancer, there is no hope." My father echoed pensively, "No hope." Dejected, I thought the same. My uncle was only forty-five or forty-six years old.

On the 16th, my mother paid him a casual visit. She came back and told me he might not last until the next month. On the morning of the 18th, I went to visit him, taking some tangerines and apples. He was still unaware he had cancer.

I took the tram to Aoyama and changed to the one bound for Akabanebashi at Aoyama 1-chome station. The weather was unusually warm, and I thought to myself, "Spring is almost here." When I boarded the Akabanebashi tram, there was just one empty seat. I sat down and, as I did so, took a close look at the woman opposite. She was about thirty years of age but had already lost her bloom, with dark circles around her eyes. She appeared to have led a rough life. Yet she was not unattractive. Her eyebrows were beautifully arched above her big eyes. Her tightly closed mouth was also appealing. I was a little troubled by the gourd-like shape of her face, but concluded she must have been very beautiful five or six years ago. Looking at her, I felt my lips drawn to hers. I knew the sweetness of a kiss from my dreams—knew it only to the extent that a hungry child imagines the sweetest persimmon in someone else's garden. Even if Tsuru did not exist, though, I would never dream of wanting to marry such a woman.

I had come to visit my dying uncle, yet I was still thinking such foolish thoughts. I got off the tram and hurried to the hospital.

As I passed through the corridors, the fragrance of medicine and the white figures of the nurses brought it home to me where I was. I was still thinking about my uncle's illness, but could not imagine him sleeping in his hospital room. I could only think of intangible things such as illness and death.

My aunt was away on business. An attendant gave me permission to enter the room.

My uncle looked much thinner than he had a few weeks before.

He lay on his back in pain. His face was bony, his skin yellowish. He was clearly dying. He looked up at me and thanked me for coming.

Then, extending his hand, he pinched some of his flabby skin and showed me, laughing at how skinny he had become.

At that moment, Tolstoy's *The Death of Ivan Ilyich* came to my mind. I recalled how, when Ilyich had fallen ill and was dying, the comforting words people spoke only distressed him. A young servant gave him some comfort by telling him the truth. I was ashamed that I could not love my uncle with the same sincerity as that young servant, but had no choice other than try as best I could to say something to ease his mind.

"If only the weather would improve," I said, "I'm sure you would be able to recover your lost weight in no time."

He said, "I don't mind being thin, but it is dreadful not wanting to eat anything."

He must have realized he was probably going to die. Even so, he must also have fancied he would go on living. It was unbearable to watch.

Overcome with compassion, I wished there was something I could do for him. I felt the closeness of death even now. I too would die one day. It was hard to remain there for so long, saying things to ease his mind. Each time my uncle said something hopeful, I felt ashamed.

"When the cherry blossoms bloom, let's celebrate my recovery and make some noise, eh!" he said cheerfully, with a wry smile. Then looked at me as if waiting for a reply. He was trying to work out if I believed his words or not. I only laughed and said yes. Forcing something more would only make it worse. I stayed for about thirty minutes, then farewelled him cheerfully and left the room. It was unendurable.

I knew the fear of death from my dreams. There is nothing in the world more hateful than that fear. Nothing is more horrifying than death. My uncle had to face this dreadful, dreadful thing day after day, which is an unbearable thought. Yet even at the moment of death, we are given the power to fantasize about the possibility of survival. Fancies may be shattered by the real world. But new ones arise like the heads of a hydra, cut after cut. This is often the only place to which to retreat. My uncle would probably sometimes escape to this hiding place. At least I tried to do everything in my power that day to help him find refuge.

By the time I left the hospital gate and turned right, the sunlight and scent of early spring filled me with contentment. My heart, which had been contracted by the visit with my uncle, began to feel more relaxed. As a moralist, I felt compassion for him, but reasoned that it was the work of nature.

I wanted to be nursed by Tsuru when it came my time to die. Then it would not be so bad even to die young.

What was going to happen about Tsuru? I did not know if things between her and me would turn out well, though I was hopeful. I pictured my uncle. Even stronger than the distress his image stirred in my heart, was the feeling it would be unlucky to think about Tsuru at this moment.

(My uncle passed away on the 20th of March.)

8

Another few days had passed since I visited my uncle.

Not a day went by without thinking about Tsuru. Only when I was with her did I feel whole. I wished she were there with me to enjoy anything I read or saw. When I was happy, lonesome, or sad, saw beautiful things, or ate good food, I wished we were together.

My father, mother, brother, sister-in-law, niece, and friends are all admirable people. My friends often tell me: "There is no one so fortunate as you." Absolutely so, but I need someone to love me even more, someone to return my passion. I am hungry for a woman.

A year or two ago I told a friend of mine in Azabu that it would be terrifying to marry Tsuru. Yet I would like to experience the joy of that terror and to savor it without sacrificing my own destiny.

For five years I have longed for this joy. She must share my love for her. Just as I dreamed of the time when we could become husband and wife, she would share the same dream.

Certainly Mr. Kawaji would soon have something to say.

Anxious and full of hope, I waited for his message. He had likely already gone to Tsuru's house. He may not have informed me because he did not consider it pressing. Or else, perhaps he had other business and had not been yet. Or then again, it was possible the delay was so he could give me the final decision at her home. Being naively optimistic, I believed this was most likely the fact of the matter.

It was the evening of March 2, when the letter from Mr. Kawaji arrived. Praying for good fortune, and with a burning sense of anxiety and hope, I cut the seal. Then read, and my anger started to rise.

Mr. Kawaji met with Tsuru's father and they discussed various issues, but her father insisted that she was still young and her brother had not yet taken a bride. He said she had received marriage proposals from other men, including a medical doctor and the son of a moneybags with a massive fortune, but he had rejected them all with the same answer. Mr. Kawaji wished he could have argued my case more vigorously, but had not wanted to jeopardize the proposal. His reply to me was rather hazy.

In his letter, Mr. Kawaji continued that he would try to work out a better approach, but it was advisable to wait for the time being.

Summoning all my strength, I tried to inspire myself. *I am a Brave Warrior, a Brave Warrior,* over and over. Yet somehow the tears came. It was hopeless. Nothing to be done. Around ten o'clock I went to bed. Then wept.

After some hours I fell into a fitful sleep, until about one in the morning. Feeling a powerful sense of self-pity, I opened my eyes. Unable to bear it, I got up and wrote in my diary.

The 3rd

Awoke at around one o'clock.

The misery. Too much of a disaster to bear. Wracking my brains for an answer to no avail, I wept.

I have thought of her every single day for five years, and now suffer the consequence. This is my own fault, no one else's, yet I despair, having come this far.

I started loving her in September of the thirtieth year of Meiji [1897]. Three and a half years have passed, during which I never stopped wanting — no, needing — to marry her.

Behind it all lay my belief that it was for her benefit and that she desired the same thing.

I must be a fool to be so conceited.

It took nineteen months to elicit my parents' consent. I put myself through such suffering.

I gained the deepest sympathy of my family, Mr. Kawaji, and my friends. It is wonderful to receive their support. I have a tranquil countenance and often enjoy a calm state of mind, but how often have I wept, has my heart been crushed, have I despaired, because of all this!

If Tsuru has no sympathy for me, I would prefer to abstain from any marriage arrangements.

Her father is probably the one most unsympathetic towards the dialogue. If Tsuru wanted to do something about it, however, then her father would probably find himself able to proceed.

She seems to lack any care for me.

If I had none for her, I would not want her to be my wife and would have no wish to become her husband, particularly if it meant annoying so many people in the process. To be so naively optimistic and good-natured would only be self-indulgent.

If she finds no joy in becoming my wife, then I find none in being her husband.

I would not want such a woman to be my wife, one who is unwilling to have me as a husband. I am not such a greedy man as to be content with that.

I need to know Tsuru's heart.

She should already know who I am. If she does not feel the slightest sympathy for me despite knowing I am in such distress and does not want to rescue me, then she is not fit to be my wife.

If she loves and commiserates with me but knowing her own weakness remains silent, then she is a wretched individual.

She is a pitiable human being, and for as long as I perceive her as such, I will not think of her at all.

That makes me feel like a man again. It would seem best not to give her another thought.

Even if this is a mistaken way of thinking, then regardless, I will not even think of her, in order to prove it to myself.

I need to know her heart.

You will never know her heart, she is enslaved. Entrusts her destiny to her father and brother, believing it beneficial.

She thinks it wicked to give herself over to her passions.

A woman with no selfhood, no ego.

A woman without ego lacks the courage to share the secrets of her heart with others. I have no opportunity to hear them, but it must be just as impossible for anyone else.

However, I do want to hear her secret thoughts. Women are generally quite bold about such issues. Their whole life depends on them. Even if I could ask, though, Tsuru's response would probably, in her impotence, be a poor one.

There is nothing else to do but anxiously wait things out. But I cannot bear it any more. I have endured too much.

I need to know if she loves me or not, because then I will be able to give up, and my anxiety will not have been in vain.

(Night, 2:10 a.m.)

My head felt a little rested after writing all this in my diary, so I went to bed, but woke up again still agitated and, in tears, wrote the following new-style poem under the title "Happily Ever After."

Make up your mind!
End this constant despair,
These ceaseless thoughts of her.

What a weakling!
A woman loved by so many men
Cannot think of only you!

So cowardly!
It's not that you want to give her up,
You are just too weak to do it.

Be a man
And give her up like a man,
She who neither loves nor cares for you.

Give up on her . . .
Does she not love me?
Care for me not?

Till the truth of that be known,
I will not give up,
But it is because I choose not to.

Three times I woo her
And thrice her father forbids —
How can I believe she loves me still?

Her father's words
Are too weak
To make me change my mind.

How fortunate!
Truly fortunate indeed,
More than you think.

I will not abandon her,
Bring her unhappiness and pain,
But be proudly steadfast.

I am simply amazed!
At a loss for words!
Indeed, indeed!

Hearing your wisdom
Fortunate, fortunate!
So it is indeed!

So very fortunate,
Enough to torment others and myself,
Fortunate, fortunate!

9

I went to Kugenuma Pavilion the next day, which was March 4. There were few patrons, because the spring holidays were still a few days away. I occupied a sunny room on the second floor, which had a view of Enoshima.

I wanted to come here to nourish my courage. It was best to leave everything about Tsuru to Kawaji and fate, and not think about them at all, but to keep my body and thoughts sound. I was becoming a little too neurotic these days.

Walking around the beaches and fields for four days, I read as little as I could. On the fifth day, I returned home.

After that, I tried as hard as I could not to think about Tsuru, but I could not help myself. Then, at some point on the fifteenth or sixteenth of March, I started once again to have the feeling we would marry.

I still believed she yearned for me, and moreover, that fate would join us together as husband and wife.

Why? I can only answer "Why not?" I am a man of reason, but I somehow believe in this irrationality. Perhaps not fully, but to some extent.

Though my feelings are impossible to explain, the year before last, I tried to do so in the form of a short statement, which ends as follows:

. . . I thought it was because of her passionate love for me, though her behavior did not seem to indicate anything of the sort. It seemed as though at least she did not quite dislike me, but may not quite love me either. In this way, she does not seem a particularly ardent woman. I forced myself to imagine that if we were unable to marry, I would become desperate and kill myself, even though she did not seem to be particularly suitable. She is an old-fashioned, womanly woman, one who would go wherever her family commanded. This would be far too weak a reason for me to marry her.

In any event, I now have a passionate love for her, and my only wish is to be married to her. I can only say I have the feeling that I must.

To me, this is not a meaningless feeling, perhaps because, although I do not even want to think about her, I cannot help doing so. That is just the way I think and I am unable to stop.

The facts are these. I sometimes meet a seventeen or eighteen-year-old woman in my neighborhood, an elegant, beautiful, solitary, seemingly affectionate, and quite vivacious woman. I have never spoken to her, even to say hello. Even though I did not know her name, since I was fifteen or sixteen, every time we encountered each other, we exchanged glances, and for some time now I have had feelings for her. I have loved her since the year before last. Now more than ever, we need morally to be together.

I had never experienced anything like it before. I felt unqualified for marriage with others whom I have loved. But this time love commands me to marry her.

Underlying my dilemma seems to exist an insistence by nature, which is at the same time a deep and mysterious indication by my soul. It is like a sign, a mystical pronouncement: "Marry her, and you shall have the greatest assistance in your work. And so shall your offspring be born the favored children of nature."

This is my superstition and to me it seems true, that is all. As in Onatsu-san's story of love and lost love, is it not fate's way of binding Tsuru and me together?[1]

So far in life, I may have done some lowly things, but I have never disobeyed nature's tacit revelations. I have even learned recently to understand these natural directives to some extent.

Indeed, I am afraid not to follow my superstitious beliefs. I have not told my father or mother about this. They would laugh at me if I did. But it is my own individual thinking. Even if it means offending my father and mother for the present, I will follow my beliefs. I do not wish to defy my parents, but I can still redeem myself. Above all, the most dangerous thing is to resist nature.

I wonder whether my superstition is really a superstition at all? Would it please my parents if it were not? That would be a huge thing.

Therefore, even though my parents may think me selfish and ignorant, I will not marry anyone else until I have proposed to Tsuru and she has refused.

It is best to follow my superstitious belief and nature's advice as far as possible, and if I do not succeed, then there will be simply nothing more I can do about it.

It is wrong for the shallow human intellect to test nature, but I want to know whether my belief is mere superstition or not.

If someone were to say to me, "You are only inventing a fanciful theory because you want to marry her," then I would have no choice but to remain silent.

With the ability to hold onto this superstition, I can forever have hope that Tsuru and I will one day be united by fate.

In the beginning it may have been a struggle to hang onto hope, without my realizing it. But over the course of five years, hope has become habitual. No matter what comes along to deny it, no matter how many reasons arise to refute it, I am certain that Tsuru and I will become husband and wife before I know it.

10

I awoke early on the morning of April 1. It was a pleasant day with fine weather. I went to look at the newspaper box. My heart was unusually agitated.

I knew that on April 1 there would be a graduation ceremony at Tsuru's school. The year before last, I had seen Tsuru go to school wearing a hat with her school crest. Wondering what the occasion might be, I saw her come home in the evening, still wearing the hat. I thought then that she must have graduated. The same day, the *Asahi Shimbun* newspaper published the names of nine of her schoolmates who had won honors. Her name was not among them.

Tsuru was not very good at school, was she? Well, it was perhaps fortunate she was not a brilliant student, for if she graduated with honors, she would attract the attention of others who might want to take her as a wife. Although, happily, she was no honors student, she continued to attend once school started. She must not have graduated after all, which was why she had not been on the list.

Later I heard from Mr. Kawaji about Tsuru's grades at

school. I was proud she had achieved such good results. On April 1 last year, the *Asahi Shimbun* reported the names of more than a dozen honors graduates from her school. Since I knew she was graduating the following year, however, I paid no attention.

The year came when she would graduate. I got up early on April 1 and went to check the newspaper. It had not yet arrived. I walked around the garden in the morning air, not wanting to miss the bell. After a while it rang. Despite feeling anxious and somehow embarrassed, I went immediately to see.

The results were indeed out. Tsuru's name was fourth among the one hundred and three graduates. I smiled to myself, I was so proud.

At that moment, I recalled that when I graduated from the Peers' School, I came fourth out of thirty or so who graduated.[1] Amused by the coincidence, I smiled even more.

My father and mother read the newspaper but did not notice Tsuru's name. Around one o'clock, I went to my mother's room and casually mentioned that Tsuru had graduated with honors.

She said indifferently, "Yes, I see," and added, "She has done quite well." Feigning nonchalance, I said, "It would seem so." My mother again said, "I hope that your proposal will be decided soon. There are not many good prospects about these days. You are all I worry about."

When I think that my mother is indifferent to this matter, I make it seem as if I am worried that things will not be settled. But when she says this to me, I say: "There is no need to worry about me. There are few people in the world who have less need to be worried about than I do."

"That may be, yet there are many things I have to tell you, to help prepare you," she said. I was glad to hear this and smiled involuntarily. I believed that things would work out between Tsuru and her. I had worried at times because of my mother's initial reluctance to receive Tsuru. Now she seemed willing to go along with the idea.

Still, I could not be certain that it would all go well.

That evening, I visited a friend in Hayabusachō. While we were conversing about various things, he told me about something interesting he had found the night before.

"I was searching for a copy of the magazine *Jugend* that contains a good sketch by Fidus," he said, and showed me an old issue.[2] I opened it to see the sketch.

A glimpse of a boat amid raging waves, carrying a young man and woman. She strains to control the tiller, while staring towards their destination. Her disheveled hair flails in the wind, and the man rows with all his might. In short, the two are locked in a frantic attempt to reach their goal, and the vigor of their efforts is palpable.[3]

What is their destination? *Zur Brautinsel*: To the bridal island.

"Not bad, is it?" said my friend.

"Excellent," I replied.

But looking at the drawing, I was thinking of myself and my beloved. I thought about Tsuru and my desire to marry her. I envied the couple in the drawing. How happy I would be if Tsuru devoted herself resolutely to our marriage, just like the woman in this picture. I pretended to be admiring the picture while thinking this sort of thing to myself.

Then, "Yes, very good indeed, this Fidus pencil sketch," I said, as if I had just reached a considered conclusion.

"Truly masterful and with great character," my friend said.

As I continued to admire the picture, I had the thought that if Tsuru did not love me, then my efforts would be ridiculous. I envied this couple even more. They probably have many enemies, but when you work assiduously for your goal, there is no doubt you will achieve it. The results of your efforts will be evident. You encourage and help each other. You can trust in your tender passion for each other.

I could not help but envy them.

How happy I would be if Tsuru truly loved me and strove sincerely to be my wife. That would make it all worthwhile.

I put down the Fidus picture, and my friend and I discussed other things.

Occasionally I looked at the picture and thought about Tsuru. How was she? What did she think of me? Certainly a nasty, shameless, impudent man. A snakelike person. This I thought over and over again.

So doing, I stayed with my friend until eleven o'clock.

Zur Brautinsel (1893) by FIDUS (Hugo Höppener)

11

I have not seen her for more than a year now and may never see her again. If I do, it will be as a bride-to-be.

I often think so. I muse about Tsuru growing up and becoming more mature and beautiful, but I cannot picture her as an adult. Sometimes I wonder if she will become ill. Or I wonder if she may be injured. I imagine her becoming ugly and crippled. Then I would kneel before her and say, "I love you. Will you be my wife?" I adore her gorgeous face. But even more than that, I love her character.

Just the same, when I think of this, I can't help but recall a time ten years ago, when I was smitten by a good-looking man of my own age, a truly attractive individual. Many students strove to win his heart. I fantasized about him unexpectedly becoming ugly. I would kneel before him when others abandoned him, and say, "I adore you with all my heart," and be pleased he had lost his looks. At the time, I believed I was drawn to his inner nature. But as the man aged, he did indeed grow increasingly ugly. As he became unsightly, I found I could no longer love him, and I began to notice the flaws in his character as well.

From what my father and Mr. Kawaji have told me, Tsuru is a person of high repute among everyone. She seems to be too good a woman to be true. She is just as reflected in my own eyes, and indeed, her neighbors, friends, and teachers all praise her. She receives nothing but compliments. It was because she was beautiful, that I yearned for her. There are others who surpass her in beauty, and not only in beauty. But I would not have thought so much of her if she had been ugly, or not better than average. It would be fearful if she became ugly. Yet even if she were to become hideous, I would not abandon her but would still be overjoyed to marry her. At first I loved her countenance and appearance, but now I believe that I love Tsuru herself, aspects of her that the eye cannot see. Still, it is her beauty for which I long — long for fervently — though I fear it attracts the attention of other men. She must undoubtedly have already attracted the attention of a great many. Tsuru's father said that she had abstained from other marriage proposals as well.

I wanted to know what had happened to her, and as a matter of fact, the gods of fate granted me this wish on May 12.

It was a Wednesday, a day off for my friend in Nakano. Since the weather was good, at around 8:00 a.m. I abruptly decided to pay him a visit. I left immediately and arrived at his house at around nine o'clock. We talked for a while and then went for a walk, passing through the green fields of wheat and sundry trees, surveying the clear sky and the black soil. I was nostalgic for this semi-rural atmosphere, having lived in the city for so long.

I said to him, "One day, I think I'd like to buy a house in Nakano, too."

"By all means, please do," he replied. Then, as though the thought just struck him, "Has anything happened with your situation?"

"Things are much the same," I said, "but I have a feeling it will all work out."

"You seem rather doubtful," he said.

"I've already done all I can. It can't be helped."

"I have a feeling it will go smoothly for you."

"I have the same feeling, but the result will probably be the opposite."

Saying this, I felt lonely. If only Tsuru were here beside me instead of he.

I changed the subject. I stayed with him until about 11:30, when I headed home. He saw me to the Nakano tram stop. The tram had not arrived, and I wished it never would. I could not help but imagine myself sharing a tram with Tsuru, on my way to and from my friend's home in Nakano. It made me happy to imagine that the longer I waited for the tram, the greater would be my chance of running into her.

Before long the tram arrived. I bade my friend farewell, boarded, and took a seat a little further than halfway back. The tram departed a short time later. I had thought that Tsuru might be waiting at the tram stop, but then realized that since it was now about twelve o'clock, she would probably be having her lunch. Here I was looking forward, as usual, to arriving in Ōkubo. The tram stopped for a moment at Kashiwagi and then departed. My chest tightened, which was not unusual. I had experienced the same feeling dozens of times here, but only once had I met her, on April 4 last year.

As the tram pulled into Ōkubo, I looked anxiously at the platform, where six or seven people stood waiting. Among them was a young woman. I wondered if it might be Tsuru, as the tram crawled to a stop.

It was Tsuru! She seemed to recognize me momentarily. She was about to get in through the rear door, but her foot suddenly halted. She pulled back and got in from the front. We looked at each other eye to eye. Her face blushing, she sat down on the right-hand side of my seat, with three people between us.

I was surprised at how she had matured. She was wearing a plain kimono, as ever, and thinly applied white face powder. I had never seen such a beautiful woman.

Gentle, beautiful, with an expressive countenance, lively eyes, red lips, and a wonderful complexion. If only I could see her face more clearly, but others were in the way. I could see only a lock of red hair (Tsuru has red hair).[1] Beside me was a laborer. Next to him was a soldier, then a woman about 40 years old, and across from her sat Tsuru.

I was sorry that she had not taken the empty seat across from me. Flustered at our seeing each other unexpectedly, she had been too embarrassed.

There were quite a few people in Shinjuku. In Yoyogi, there were so many that the place was almost full. If only an elderly person would get on board, or someone carrying a child. Then I would be able to stand up discretely, the better to see Tsuru. But there was a man standing in front of me.

A few passengers got off at Sendagaya. At Shinanomachi, five or six got off, and then three or four more. Shortly before reaching Yotsuya, I stood up and looked at Tsuru. Our eyes met, but she immediately looked away. I decided to move forward and stop in front of her. The tram was slowing, but she did not stand up. She turned her face away from me, and the tram did indeed come to a stop. I started to pass in front of her, and at this moment, she suddenly rose. Wonderful! My hand brushed against Tsuru's back. I followed her and was about to step off the tram. At this moment, a man with a child stood up by the entrance. I did not dare to push him aside and follow directly after Tsuru, but left the two of them between us.

I got behind them, then tried to follow Tsuru through the ticket gate. But as she went through she looked back and saw me. She moved her body nonchalantly to the right as if to beckon me to go through first. Taking the initiative, I went through ahead of her, with a husbandly authority, though my heart was not in it. As I was about to give my ticket to the ticket gate attendant, I dropped it. I looked as it fell out of my hand and watched the attendant pick it up. After exiting the station, I turned right and climbed the stairs on the left-hand side, then I turned around to see Tsuru again. After climbing a flight of stairs, I looked around to see her coming up after me on the left side.

I turned around again before reaching the top. Tsuru was still following the course I had taken. I climbed up further and turned right to go towards Kōjimachi Street. When I turned around again, I saw that she had finished climbing the stairs and was still trailing me. I was elated, delirious.

I felt such an intimacy with her that I wanted to call out, "Tsuru-san!" Even when I did so, she was not startled, but responded almost laughingly:

"Is there something I can do for you?"

I slowed down. I was on the left side of Kōjimachi Street, following the tram track. She was walking on the right side of the street, not following the track.

I turned my head I do not know how many times, and each time our gazes met. Flustered, I looked again at where I was going. She also seemed to avert her gaze.

She loves me! My heart thrilled with joy.

Sincerity engenders sincerity. Just as I loved Tsuru, so she loved me.

My feet lurched and moved faster. When I came to Rokuchōme, I turned around but could no longer see her. Perhaps she was in a store, but I could not see her. Unbearably happy, I hurried home.

Tsuru loves me! She will be my wife. We were born destined to be a married couple.

Certainly this was a happy day, one to commemorate. Tsuru must be just as pleased. I could not help returning home joyously. I went to see my mother. "Today I saw Tsuru! She is so beautiful. I can't express how much more beautiful Tsuru is than Manryū!" I wanted to say. My mother had seen the famous geisha Manryū one day and admired her beauty.[2] She had not remarked on Tsuru's beauty when, three years ago, I pointed her out as she passed in front of our window.

So, I felt uneasy about sharing the incident with my mother. Even after lunch, I was unable to settle down and went out to Kanda. I could not stop smiling and thinking about Tsuru. Beautiful, beautiful, gentle, gentle, noble, noble, Tsuru is woman!

That evening, I visited my friend in Azabu and said simply, "I met Tsuru!" He said, "Well, that must have been nice, mustn't it?"

12

After I met her on May 12, I felt that Tsuru and I would finally become husband and wife. Then I wondered about what would happen after that.

We would be happy forever. It was simply unimaginable that life could become humdrum for us, as it usually did for ordinary married couples. We would be modest in our carnal desires and united in our mutual appreciation and love for each other, rendering any discord impossible. I am aware that more experienced people will scoff at such thoughts, calling them young and self-delusional. There is no one in the world more annoying than people like this who pose as teachers, taking it for granted that the young, with their own experience upon which to rely, will follow the path they have taken. Such people will be amazed when they discover that I have an ideal marriage and family. I will not consider my wife to be a mere plaything, as they do. A woman who is with child will naturally become less lovely and even suffer from hysteria. I am completely sympathetic and will be truly loving and tender. I will uproot sources of unhappiness that they are unable even to see. I will demonstrate that Tsuru's and my love is of a totally different order to their own.

While it may take many forms, a true love between a man and woman is eternal and immortal.

If Tsuru's and my love could ever end in misfortune—I would truly want to investigate how it might be possible.

Though others will probably ridicule me for marrying her, such ridicule will eventually turn to envy and respect, for ours will be the model of an ideal marriage.

There is no greater love than my love for her, a love that considers our intellectual destiny, work, and personalities. In fulfilling our love, we will learn many things, hidden mysteries.

There was now little doubt we were going to become man and wife. Whether sooner or later was the only question. As one might expect, however, sometimes I experienced misgivings, momentary doubts. Then at some point, for no particular reason at all, I would arrive once again at the understanding that everything would turn out well.

Through May and June, I waited in vain for good news from Mr. Kawaji, and then again through July and August. I had been in Tokyo all summer, and at the beginning of September, I went to Senbonhama in Numazu. When I returned home after a week's stay there, I was expecting a reply saying that he had finally received news from Tsuru's family. I anticipated his return, but September also passed with nothing.

One day in October, I was walking in the garden, deeply breathing in the lonely autumn air, when a maid came to me. She handed me a letter.

My heart leapt into my throat. It was from Mr. Kawaji.

I cut the seal and read. I summoned all my strength, while my eyes filled with tears.

Tsuru had become a married woman.

I tried to bear it but could not, and I cried out aloud, not knowing what to do. I walked around the garden in a daze, then went into my room and wept on the desk.

Tsuru was the wife of the eldest son of a wealthy Kashiwagi resident, who had become an engineer that year.

13

After that, I tried to eject her from my imagination and into the storehouse of my memory. However, it was a lonely and painful effort, as well as a futile one. There was nothing to do but leave things in the hands of time.

Wandering around in a flower garden from which all the flowers had been taken away, I mocked myself and my lonely heart.

I who hunger for a woman may love one again some day, and the time may come when I will celebrate my present loss of love. But such a thought could do nothing for me now. I knew nothing but misery. My heart was broken.

Perhaps I might go on a trip, I considered. If I did not travel I would break down. But I am a brave warrior. It should be a blessing and not a misfortune if a woman who did not love me were to become someone else's wife. I should be glad I did not marry her. I am not the kind of person who, having suffered an unrequited love and the consequences of my own actions, is afraid of doing something rash. Having done everything in my power, I would now accept my fate philosophically.

I decided to stay in Tokyo. I hid my loneliness and put on a brave face. My father, mother, and Mr. Kawaji must have wished they had not had to worry so much about trying to get me married.

But how may we endure, except in the knowledge that we have done all we are able? Is that not some comfort? The only consolation for a mother who has lost her beloved child is the knowledge that she has done all she possibly could to save it.

On the evening of November 3, I visited a friend of mine who had graduated in engineering that year. I casually asked him about Tsuru's husband. He knew him well and said he was a likable and energetic man with a good physique. My friend even told me that the fellow was delighted to have recently married a beautiful, loving wife.

I said casually, "I see," and when he finished the story, my friend suddenly asked me why I wished to know. My face flushed and I weakened, as though I might start to weep.

I said something incomprehensible like, "Just something I wanted to ask you."

He was not in any hurry to get to the bottom of it.

After a while I began to believe, without any reason, that Tsuru had actually loved me, but married someone else unwillingly, at the urging of her father, mother, and older brother. Another month passed, and I began to feel a sense of pity for her and then to worry about her fate.

I wanted to see her and ask if this feeling of mine was true or not.

However, even if she said, "I have never thought about you," it would be no more than just words. It would only be in her mind.

February 43rd year of Meiji [1910]

End of main narrative

Supplementary Record

*To be understood as written by
the protagonist of* The Innocent

Two People (from my book *The Wilderness*)

1

There were a male and a female, who were both at an age when they were beginning to know love. They may possibly have seen each other before. No, I am certain of it. He was thirteen, she ten, and they had met in the street. At that time, the boy thought she was lovely, and she found him splendid. But the two of them forgot all about it. They did not even dream of it again. Their houses were only a block and a half away from each other.[1]

Of course, they had never spoken, they did not know each other's name, and to begin with, the boy was not even aware that the girl existed in this world, nor was she aware that he did. But was there no relation between them? Was there no connection, something they were unaware of?

The woman that the man has in his mind as his ideal woman is that very one. He can be named, for argument's sake, Ichirō, and the woman, Shizu. If the ideal woman that Ichirō had in his mind was created and made into a living woman, it would surely be Shizu. If, hypothetically, an omniscient and omnipotent god had created Shizu's ideal man, would it not be Ichirō who came into being?

These two are not artists and cannot imagine an ideal person's face. They are not sculptors and do not know an ideal person's skeleton. They are not poets and are unable to envisage the nature of an ideal person. However, these two have something they yearn for, and that is, for Ichirō, Shizu, and for Shizu, Ichirō.

Those times that Ichirō longs for someone and is lonely, Shizu also has a yearning and is lonely as well.

When Shizu spontaneously becomes happy, Ichirō also becomes happy without reason. There must be something between the two of them. It was as though one of them emitted a sound of a certain vibration, and the other would do the same without even knowing it. This is just how it was between them.

It would happen without their knowing, mysteriously, and they never wondered why they would suddenly feel lonely or happy.

One day they happened to meet in the street. Ichirō thought she was lovely, and Shizu found him handsome. They fell in love on the spot, but neither would ever know it. Ichirō wondered why he could not get Shizu out of his head, and Shizu thought the same thing about him. They tried to forget each other, but the harder they tried, the more they were reminded. They were frustrated with their own lack of willpower.

That night, although each thought they were trying to forget the other, both were overcome with a joyful anxiety, as if having tasted of forbidden fruit. Both had strict families, and so they felt ashamed and guilty about their desires.

They did not know each other's name or where they lived. Even when each tried to recall the other's appearance, they could not bring it to the surface. Yet neither of them could forget. Their longing grew stronger. They used to long for someone without knowing why, but now, although they still did not know why, what they longed for has assumed form. The one longed-for has risen into consciousness.

Of course, they found this neither appropriate, beautiful, or natural. They never dreamed they were resonating with each other.

Subsequently, they went at the same time to that place, two or three times. The reason was that when Ichirō felt his vague longing, his feet guided him there, and Shizu's feet also took her there without her knowing it. But since it was something not risen into consciousness that guided them, they were prevented from meeting even a single time out of ten.

Their thinking became more intense, and both began to prefer solitary places. They brooded and were lost in thought.

Ichirō tried to reinvigorate himself, berating himself for having become so effete. Shizu also wondered why she was thinking about that young man so much, reproached herself, and tried to forget him. But it was to no avail, and they yearned and became nostalgic, desolate, and teary-eyed. Aha! It must be they are in love, and beloved. Sometimes they even smile to themselves. They look happy one moment and sad the next. They were afraid that others would realize, and they felt ashamed and embarrassed.

If this were a conscious thing, they would have been able to overpower it. But their yearning and nostalgia originated outside their consciousness. "Why is it so strong?" was a question they could neither ask nor answer themselves.

One day, when Shizu was absent-mindedly sitting at her desk, her mother anxiously asked her, "What has come over you recently? Is something the matter?" She answered indifferently, "No," but when her mother left, she grew sad and cried at her desk, feeling she should have told her about her feelings. After a while, she regained her composure and left the house alone to go to the usual place. Inadvertently, she met Ichirō. Their eyes met, then parted, then met again, then parted again. They passed by each other in a daze, both taking a few erratic steps. Ichirō nervously turned his head, and Shizu tried to resist the urge to do the same. She pretended to look at something outside, and when she turned around again she could see only the back of his head.

The two felt happy, but they could not be sure they loved each other. They had never opened their hearts to each other, nor even spoken eye to eye. They did not know what their hearts could say to each other. They were happy but felt lonely and sad at the same time.

And so a year passed, and two years.

They think of each other fondly, but their love remains in doubt.

They may have talked eye to eye several times over the course of two years, and even heart to heart, but they do not know each other's name, nor their family, nor their heart.

2

Two years is a long time for someone afflicted with yearning. Ichirō thought about telling his father or mother about his feelings, but he had not yet entered university, and did not know if the girl loved him or not, so how could he tell them he loved her? He didn't know anything about the girl and had never even spoken to her. He agonized and kept it secret in his heart to avoid being ridiculed.

From time to time, Shizu also thought about confiding in her mother, but neither did she know the boy's name nor what he was like, and it would be embarrassing to try to explain her feelings about someone with whom she had no more contact than occasionally passing him in the street. In agony, she kept it to herself, thinking that if she did tell her mother, what difference could it possibly make?

Sometimes, the two would pray to the gods, but without conviction. Why should the gods grant them time to hear about what they themselves thought may be no more than a nagging infatuation? The more they thought about it, the more they felt they should dismiss it, but since it was not something they were fully conscious of, they could not forget, either. They tried various means to distract themselves, but some unknown thing was searching for them and would eventually embrace them, sooner or later.

The two pretended to be cheerful if only to please their parents, but that made them even lonelier. On moonlit nights, they wandered through their gardens in tears, never dreaming that someone else, a neighborhood and a half away, was suffering as well. No one doubts the possibility of communicating at a distance by telephone, but one cannot communicate what has not risen into one's consciousness.

It is hard to believe they were not in love with each other, but they put it down to infatuation and, unreasonably, willfully, consoled themselves with this thought. To reiterate, they had no idea how to speak heart to heart, eye to eye. They had no wish to occupy themselves with anything beyond their studies.

Each believed that the next time they met, they would be able to discern whether the other one loved them or not, but when they happened to meet by chance they would be startled and forget all of that. It was only after the other had passed by that each would regain their senses. Another year went by.

Shizu turned nineteen, an age when her mother and father turned their attention to the matter of her marrying. However, the situation between her and Ichirō remained the same. The clearer it became that each loved the other, the more they doubted that the other loved them in return, and the more they contemplated, the more confused they became, until each began to doubt the other's merits. Their stupidity became so apparent that they sometimes scoffed at themselves. When they brought these feelings to the forefront of their rational mind, they must have blushed and forgotten about them.

One day, Shizu received a marriage proposal. She refused it, but not for any particular reason. She could not see any justification for refusing. Her parents considered it a good proposal, but since their beloved daughter did not wish to go ahead with it, they decided to abstain. Later Shizu felt she had been foolish. It would have been better to have taken a little more time to consider the suitor rather than decline straight away. She had not done so because she disliked him, but because she was preoccupied with Ichirō. She had no illusion of uniting with Ichirō, but there was something she did not understand, and because of that something she had abstained from the proposal without giving it enough thought. Reflecting on it now, she could not help feeling that she had done something regrettable.

Then three or four months later came another proposal. This time her father was more amenable to it than before. But once more, without reason, Shizu was unwilling. Her father told her about this suitor's good social standing, his education, and his earnestness. She believed all that her father said and knew that he was right in wanting her to proceed. However, for some reason or another, she was again reluctant, and while she did not say so directly, her tone of voice made this clear. Fortunately, her mother checked with her fortune-teller, who told her that Shizu's age was unfavorable. When her mother said that Shizu appeared very unhappy with the arrangement, her father reluctantly bowed to them and declined the proposal. Then once again Shizu regretted what had happened. It was foolish of her to think so much about Ichirō. Why preoccupy herself so with someone to whom she had never spoken, and of whose name and character she had no idea. She herself would become old, and he would get married. . . She could not help but think herself a fool.

That September, Ichirō became a first-year law student.

They both grew impatient. She is old enough to become someone's wife, Ichirō thought, but he could not bring himself to speak up. They went to that street more often than before, but they were now under a conscious influence. When Ichirō came back in through his gate disappointed, Shizu would be leaving hers in frustration, or Shizu would go into her room to cry, just as Ichirō would be putting on his *geta* to go out and see her, and they were often at complete odds with each other. I do not love her, he does not love me, the two would sometimes lament.

And so the years passed.

3

It may seem to Ichirō as if she does not love him, but it becomes ever more difficult for him to believe that she does not love him at all. Unmistakably, that look can only mean she certainly does love him, he sometimes thinks. If that is true, then he must tell her that he wants to unite with her. The reason he does not is that he does not want to be laughed at. But if she dislikes him, even if he declares his feelings and she simply dismisses him, that does not necessarily mean that he will have annoyed her.

The reason he does not speak out is that he is afraid of people whom he does not even know. It would be stupid to abandon their happiness for fear of being ridiculed by people who do not even know him. Sometimes he wishes she would ask him to unite with her. But this is something that cannot be hoped for, and when it crosses his mind, he reviles her for hardheartedness.

Even Ichirō recognizes the unreasonableness of this.

He was a cultured young man and would sometimes compose poetry when thinking of her. One day their paths happened to cross, and looking back after she had gone by, he scolded himself for lacking the courage to declare himself. He went home and wrote in his diary.

> *The figure of your back, oh my!*
> *Watching as you move away,*
> *I transgress.*
> *O, I am an offender.*

> *An offender, O forgive me!*
> *If you know my heart*
> *Weep with me.*
> *She forgives, O my beloved!*

Thinking more about it, he realized that he was not worthy of being her husband, that he would never be able to love her enough. Strange, how he had believed until now that being with her would be the only way to save her. Now he ended up with a lonely smile on his face, at the idea of having her to himself forever, but not loving her enough.

One day, at his desk, feeling lonelier and sadder than ever before, he leaned back to catch his breath. His eyes began to well up, and his tears flowed unceasingly, as a poignant nostalgia rose in his heart. He had often felt lonely and cried alone, but never as much as at this moment. He did not know why, but after a while his tears ceased. He rinsed his face and went to the place where he usually saw Shizu, but there was no sign of her. Desperate, he went back to his room and sat down at his desk again, feeling miserable. He went for a walk to distract himself, but still could not ease his loneliness. He tried to bear up, but was on the verge of tears. The thought of Shizu came to him, and he could not expel her from his mind. Despite himself, he felt such a deep affection.

In those days, Shizu would follow her parents' advice, with the understanding that she should put aside her own desires for their sake, so she acknowledged that the time had come when she must sacrifice herself in order to please them by complying with their wish that she take a husband. She could not help but think that the man who would become her husband would be a better person than she. Of course, this belief only arose in her conscious mind.

During the next few moments, both of them were struck with agonizing pangs. To Shizu there seemed a reason for this to some extent, but Ichirō could not understand what was happening to him.

One morning he looked at the newspaper and was staggered by what he saw. It was the face of the one whom he held dear, juxtaposed with that of an unfamiliar man.

Over the next few days, he wondered whether she did not love him, but for all that, his anguish faded. Then he smiled a lonely smile. He wrote down in his diary:

She has married someone
whom I do not know.
Blessed be she!
So be it.

The happy couple.
So be it.
My congratulations!
So be it, so be it.

As he wrote, he experienced a deep loneliness a deep loneliness and broke down again.

At that same instant, Shizu smiled at her husband, hiding the loneliness she felt within.

4

Some years went by, and Ichirō also married. To most eyes, his wife was a more beautiful, more gracious woman even than Shizu.

Now, both Shizu and Ichirō each consider their own home to be a happy one. Yes, as far as they are aware, their family lives are both blissful. Shizu's husband is a good man, just as she believed him to be. Ichirō's wife is a good woman, too.

Shizu has almost forgotten all about Ichirō, and he has become all but oblivious of her. Yet there are times when the two will suddenly remember, and are thankful that they did not follow the impulses of their youth. Soon, they will no longer think of each other, reverting to a time when each was not even aware of the other. But some things that do not come into their awareness will still resonate with them, as if they are sympathetic elements.

They still feel lonely at times. They have no idea why, but each will sometimes feel a longing. When Ichirō is unexpectedly happy, it is just when Shizu is unexpectedly happy. When out of the blue Shizu suddenly turns sorrowful, that is when Ichirō turns sorrowful. The two are still in tune with each other.

Shizu loves her husband, Ichirō his wife. Nevertheless, both couples enjoy no emotional harmony beyond the sphere of consciousness. They are conscious couples, and all their conscious needs are satisfied. Fortunately, they are content with their present state, for they do not recognize the existence of the things of which they are unaware.

But even now, as these feelings and this knowledge remain beyond their grasp, the two languish in solitude; as a result, they love and adore each other.

40th year of Meiji [1907]

Long Live the Ignorant!

A young man, about eighteen years old, sits writing on a piece of paper at a desk, upon which are placed a pen and a lamp. Behind him are two figures in black suits, a man (A) and a woman (B), both of indeterminate age. On the desk there is also an alarm clock, with the hands pointing to one o'clock.

A: Dreaming of happiness.

B: He has written, "Good luck to them both."

A: "Good luck to them both" probably refers to when they will become husband and wife. Unfortunately, there is no way for a young couple to know whether or not they will be happy together after they marry.

B: He writes, "I wish to marry her, even if she makes me unhappy."

A: Perhaps so, but when unhappiness does come, will he then celebrate their marriage?

B: One cannot know until the time comes, when one sees.

A: But this young man wants to know now.

B: He writes: "It will be unbearable if we can't get married."

A: Surely he knows that, unbearable though it may well be, it is inevitable.

B: Although he knows it, he doesn't want to admit it.

A: This young man is full of hope at present, so he wants the future to come soon.

B: He is thinking about when they will become husband and wife.

A: At present he seems to believe they can become a couple.

B: It is fortunate he believes so.

A: This man thinks that if his present love is broken, he will never love again.

B: What would he say if we told him now he will have a second love?

A: Probably angry, offended, desolate. . .

B: In his dream, he would instantly erase the idea, but have a feeling he was doomed to misfortune.

A: What if I said there will come a time when that second love will be broken and he will have a third love?

B: Ignorance is bliss.

A: In other words, one may be happy in the darkness ahead!

B: His third love is also broken.

A: If he knew that when he becomes thirty he will marry a woman who repulses him more than anyone in the world, he would be so upset he would kill himself.

B: Or if he discovered that his wife is to become unattractive and stubborn. . .

A: Then, in the first year, she gives birth to a baby boy.

B: Who dies in the second month.

A: The following year she bears another baby boy.

B: And the year after, they part.

A: And the next year, he marries a beautiful wife ten years younger than himself.

B: But in the first year, she dies in childbirth.

A: The first year after that, for the first time, he purchases a geisha to keep as a mistress, and the following year she becomes his wife, having given birth to a baby girl.

B: The second year, the woman sleeps with an actor she has procured.

A: She bullies her stepchildren.

B: He detests her, beautiful and vicious as she is.

A: But then he begins to take some pleasure in life.

B: And at fifty-two years of age, the parent of five children, he leaves.

A: Two of the five girls are not his own.

B: The first child is a good-for-nothing.

A: The second sickly.

B: The third dies at the age of five.

A: The oldest daughter, fourteen.

B: The second, seven.

A: All the children are as rude and selfish as the wife.

B: He can only expect that his family will come to ruin after his death.

A: He occupies a prominent position as a man of letters until thirty-four or five, but is forgotten before very long and treated as an old man by the time he reaches forty.

B: Unaware of such things, he jots away here, optimistic and carefree. He writes, "I am a rather contented person to believe that, while I can't think that any woman would love someone like me, she certainly does, and perhaps we may become a couple. It is dreadful to think there is no one in the world as happy as I am."

A: He seems to have inscribed the word "dreadful" with only the very tip of his brush.

B: Even in his dreams he does not know that there are times when he writes, "Is there anyone in the world as unhappy as me?"

A: Let us celebrate unknowable things for the sake of this young man.

A and B: (Together.) Hurrah for ignorance!

(The young man puts down his pen and stands up.)

Young Man: Please God grant us both good fortune and make us husband and wife.

(A and B look at each other.)

End
November of Meiji 42 [1909]

What if Never Born?

"What if I had never been born?"

Toyō Nakata's head began to ache as he thought about this. He thinks of his birth as an accident, something experienced by chance, something of a miracle. But he is unable to imagine himself as he was before he was born. He was not himself before he was born, or rather, before he was conceived in his mother's womb, for then there was no such entity as himself. It seems obvious, but when he contemplates it this way, he feels a sense of pity or shame. He wants what he calls "himself" to be inevitable.

His individuality ought to have been predetermined by fate to come into existence at the precise hour and minute of May 12, 1886. Otherwise, he must regard his individuality as devoid of meaning, as if it emerged on a whim. He knew what he needed to think, but he wasn't pleased with it.

It seems to Toyō that his parent's marriage was a coincidence. The births of his mother and father were a further series of coincidences, as were those of his paternal and his maternal grandparents. It was also by chance that they married each other.

He could not help but think that of all the millions of sperm in his father's body, only a single one had come into the world, to become half his own body. The same could be said of each of his parents.

"If I had not been born, I would not be here."

Toyō tried to accept this solution, but his head spun all the more.

"I would neither have been born nor exist in the cosmos. Perhaps someone else would have been born instead. That would be the more likely scenario."

He grappled with the idea but it seemed to him far from the answer he sought. He was getting impatient.

"First of all, it is foolish to think such a thing. After all, I was born, was I not?"

He considered the proposition, but found it was not good enough.

"Just too much of an accident," he said to himself, but it did not help.

"Humanity may have significance, but individuality has none. It makes no difference whether you are born or not, it does not matter whether you live or die. It makes no great difference if you are someone else, if you are not born, and another is born instead who otherwise never would have been. Your parents will love the child as their own. Then that other child will give birth to its own child, one not born to you, and an individuality presently un-born in this world will be born instead of your offspring, who will now never come into being."

Toyō's mind was in turmoil at the notion.

He felt frustrated, like a man who had been thrown

into a riddle he was unable to solve, like someone who had tried unsuccessfully to untangle a tangled thread.

"I don't care!" he cried internally.

But his head was further muddled with a sense of regret over the still unsolved puzzle.

"If the earth had never come into being, then neither would I have been born." Unable to keep still any longer he strode agitatedly around the room.

"If I had not been born, I would never have had this thought. I would never have walked. I would never have eaten. I would not breathe, nor go to school. She may never have loved. No pain, no sorrow, no happiness or joy. There would be nothing. Yet the earth would be the same as it is now. Still, I daresay she would have been born, and in that case would have loved another man."

Toyō felt he was thinking something unthinkable, and it was arrogant of him to try solving this impossible mystery.

Impulsively, he donned his hat and went out into the street to distract himself. He saw many people who had been born with the same accidental experiences as he. Old people and children, men and women, beautiful people and ugly, fine ones and shabby, all of them walking around looking as if it were entirely natural they had been born.

Seeing this, he realized that there were many others akin to himself. He calmed down a little and went to visit his friend, who was not home, so then he went to the house of his beloved.

When she saw Toyō she burst into laughter, and he joined in. The insoluble mystery seemed to evaporate. For two hours, he lost himself in conversation with her.

On the way back home, he tried contemplating again about what things would have been like if had never been born, but it no longer seemed to matter. He was amused at himself for worrying about such a thing.

"You were born because you were born, right? If you hadn't been born, you wouldn't exist. Instead of dwelling on that, focus on how you can live a happy life!" he exclaimed silently, with a smile. Then he hurried homeward, dreaming of the future family he would create with his beloved.

October of Meiji 42 (1909)

| A Dead Friend

A: "Our acquaintance" thought himself a genius.

B: "Our acquaintance" intended to live to be eighty.

C: "Our acquaintance" wanted to create a family with his beloved.

D: He believed himself to be the happiest man alive.

A: He had been thinking about his future until the moment of death.

E: But he truly seemed to know he was going to die.

A: I wonder. . .

E: No, I believe so. When I visited him in Kamakura, "our acquaintance" gave me that lonely smile of his and said, "I'm afraid I am going to die. I feel it often these days. I try to convince myself it is not true, because I am still not working, but it doesn't do me any good. Many good people have died young. But until the moment comes, I will never believe it will happen to me, and I have never thought it would happen, not even since becoming ill with this disease."

D: That is true.

E: Then I said that it was the same for me, and laughing scornfully, he answered that it might be so, but to a different degree, that strong people are not able to be touched so acutely by the question of death, and that the matter of dying or not dying cannot dominate their minds for long.

B: Yes.

E: When he said this to me, I looked at him thoughtlessly, and seeing his skin and bones, I too realized he would die sooner or later.

A: We will all die sooner or later.

E: Please don't let's quibble. The degree is different. I had no choice other than to change the subject, so I asked him casually what it was he wanted.

A: Yes.

E: Again he laughed desolately, then enquired what it was I wanted. I asked him if he was working, and he shook his head. "What is it you want?" I asked again.

B: Yes.

E: "I want to be cared for by You-know-who," he laughed.

B: Yes.

E: I told him, "That is not in my power, I cannot do that." He said that even if it were, he would refuse. Strongly I replied, "Why?" He said, "I have pulmonary tuberculosis." He laughed and said, "If she cared for me, I would want to kiss her."

C: It's tragic, isn't it?

E: More wretched than tragic. "Our acquaintance" changed his tone of voice and said he was somewhat sad to leave this world without knowing whether she loved him or not, and now it was fortunate for her that his love had not yet been fulfilled. But unfortunate for him. "I will die without knowing the true joys of life," he said.

B: Yes.

E: I said something like, perhaps you may not die, but he only laughed scornfully and said, "Thank you, but your kindness is misplaced. I am not such an optimist, not quite such an innocent. I can see that you think I am going to die. I am only trying to talk as much as I can to remind you of who I am. I am actually quite superstitious about my own mortality. I don't want you to feel sorry for me now, for I still consider myself a hero."

B: Yes.

E: I told him that he should not let himself get angry, and if he wanted to avoid that, he should just listen to what I had to say. Then "our acquaintance" said a lot more to me.

"My greatest wish," he said, "is to be visited from time to time by my first beloved, as well as by You-know-who. The first beloved can come with her husband, and the other with her mother. I want them to visit me from time to time, without any risk to their name or well-being. I could never explain that to someone I loved. I just want to have an innocent talk, forget about death, and be happy for a time. It's good to speak to you like this. Occasionally, I feel ecstatic, but I am lonely. Moreover, I cannot help but become irrational, obsessed with death, and fall into delirium, but it's all a fantasy, something impossible. Yet I am an optimist and feel therefore that my first love, or the later one, will hear that I am dying and come to visit me." So saying, he laughed sadly.

I said, "Why not write to them?" He said, "No, I can't do that, tempting as it is. Anyway, if I did write, they would only refuse, but I wonder whether, without being asked, they might not simply come. It would be a great consolation to me when I died. Like Hannele, I might die while dreaming of the two of them."[1] And he laughed.

A: Did the two of them come to his home before he died?

E: How could they possibly?

D: I wonder whether he might have died dreaming of the two of them?

B: How can one know such a thing?

E: But I heard it was a comfortable death.

C: Surely he suffered.

A: Must have been agonizing.

B: Because he was excessively attached to life. But it's all the same when you die, isn't it?

E: Is it all the same?

B: Probably, I suppose.

End
November of Meiji 42 [1909]

| Imagination

Sister (the younger of two siblings): My brother, I read a review of your recent exhibition in today's newspaper.

Brother: (A little surprised.) Yes, it came out. What did you think of it, Kiyo?

Sister: I was delighted.

Brother: Why were you pleased to see such a scathing review?

Sister: The critic probably said such things because your works are too refined for him to understand. Reading the review made me realize how great an artist you are.

Brother: Thank you, but I found it terribly disheartening.

Sister: But why?

Brother: Because I cannot be any good if my art is seen like that.

Sister: You have said that people will be critical of your paintings when you exhibit them, because they would fail to understand their merit.

Brother: I did indeed say that, but this critic came from a totally unforeseen direction, denouncing me on points I had not anticipated. He said I was superficial, mere novelty, frivolous, trivial. I'm clumsy and don't know how to hold a brush; the colors are tasteless; it's not art. If the attack had been head on, I would have managed it. But it was from behind, from a source I did not expect. I was unsettled because the critic is well-known and impartial. If my work looks like that to him, then I begin to doubt the power of my own mind and personality.

Sister: That's not right. Surely there are others who are impressed by your paintings.

Brother: There are two types of people who admired them: close friends and dilettantes who know nothing about art.

Sister: Did you not once tell me that dilettantes understand better, because they are not trapped in dogmas?

Brother: However, they may be intimidated by ostentation.

Sister: Ostentation?

Brother: Perhaps in some of the more unconventional touches.

Sister: I used to think he was a discerning critic, because you, my brother, have praised him in the past, but after seeing this review, I believe he is rather ordinary.

Brother: What makes you say that?

Sister: He does not understand the essence of your work. He is unable to discriminate between superficial and fundamental dynamics, so he finds your paintings frivolous.

Brother: I don't believe they were. I painted every stroke with all my heart, sent all my strength into the tip of my brush. My best efforts may simply be weaker than I thought.

Sister: It's annoying how he criticizes your paintings for being fanciful or mere novelty. Where exactly are they fanciful? How merely novel?

Brother: When I painted them, I had rejected the idea of novelty. I knew I was different from others in certain ways, but had no interest in what was considered new or old. I adopted themes that were of my personality, themes to which I could devote all my strength. Whether they were novel or old-fashioned was not my concern. Still, I wonder whether the reason others see them that way is because I am not strong enough of a painter.

Sister: Nonsense, that is not true. The conclusion comes from his own coarseness. I despised him when I saw the part where he says, "Urayama is proud of his outdated paintings, thinking they have something new."

Brother: I had no such thought when I was painting, being totally immersed, but when I exhibited them, I did notice some innovative features, and felt a sense of satisfaction in them.

Sister: It is not about themes, it is an art of self expression, just as you have often said. I am proud of you for not concerning yourself with such things.

Brother: It would be nothing if I agreed with the way you see it, but I have a little more faith in those who criticize me. I doubt myself.

Sister: Why is that?

Brother: Is it not pathetic that works in which I have expressed the power of my personality so frankly can be seen as mere trivia?

Sister: This critic's preconceived notions got in his way.

Brother: I cannot consider him so obtuse.

Sister: You are wrong. He is nobody great — he knows nothing beyond the superficial.

Brother: It would be good if that were true.

Sister: The very fact that he sees your mannerisms as borrowings is proof. He is not someone who understands the fundamentals, and you ought not to doubt yourself based on criticisms made by someone like that.

Brother: But when three or four impartial people attack me in the same way, it really seems to be true, and I start to fear that my own judgment stems from egotism.

Sister: It is odd to see such a variety of people make the same sorts of criticisms as in today's newspaper. Why didn't you show me the review?

Brother: I hated the thought of your losing faith in me. **(Smiles.)**

Sister: Do you really think criticism like this would make me lose confidence in you? Do you want to deceive me into keeping my faith in you? That really is weak.

Brother: The truth is, I am strong. I despise the people who deride my paintings just as you do, but I fear it is because of my ego.

Sister: Not at all. No matter how many people malign you, I believe you will prevail in the end.

Brother: If only I could agree with you.

Sister: I'm not sure why, but I am absolutely certain that time will tell. You will feel better if we discuss ridicule of this sort.

Brother: I agree. When I don't talk about it, I am even more forlorn, believing I must be mediocre.

Sister: Why are you so afraid of the criticism of strangers?

Brother: Perhaps because I feel I'll never be able to become detached and look at myself objectively, But anyway, I suppose that is a job for a stranger.

Sister: Perhaps, but someday you will know your true value.

Brother: Sometimes that's exactly what I worry about.

Sister: Wouldn't it be best to be taken at your true value?

Brother: Yes, it's true, but perhaps I overvalue myself.

Sister: I don't know about that. Me, I think you need to value yourself more highly.

Brother: Thank you, Kiyo, you don't know how my spirits have risen now that you are here. How desolate I would be without you. How bleak it is when I lose faith in myself and you are not here. If I am ever able to paint something of enduring value, it will be thanks to you.

Sister: That is not so.

Brother: No, it really is true.

Sister: If you think that of me, I am grateful.

Brother: I am determined to follow my own path unwaveringly. Even if I have the slightest hope of success, I am going to aim for it.

Sister: You must, you really must! I am so delighted to be born the sister of a man like you.

Brother: (In tears.) I weep for joy!

Sister: (Tearfully.) So do I!

Brother: I would miss you so much if you were not here.

* * *

When he wrote this he felt better, but wept, having neither a sister nor a lover.

NOTES

1. Hibiya Moat, by the gardens of the Imperial Palace in central Tokyo. The narrative is set prior to 1910, so the term densha used here and there throughout the novel (in the present day translated as "electric train") refers to vehicles of the Tokyo Electric Tramway.
2. Throughout the narrative, the presence of the father represents a deviation from autobiographical fact: Mushanokōji's own father died when he was two years old.

CHAPTER 2

1. The meaning of the girl's name Haru is "Springtime." The "diminutive suffix" -chan attached to a person's name expresses that the speaker finds them endearing.

CHAPTER 3

1. The Kōbu private railway company commenced service in 1889 as a horse-drawn rail service. It was the forerunner of a section of the current Chūō line, and extended over a good part of Tokyo. Electrification of tramlines began in 1903, so the process was well underway by the time of the narrative (See National Diet Library Digital Collections Database, Tokyo). In Chapter 6, Jibun (meaning "I"/"me"/"myself" in the original Japanese text) mentions 1907 as being the current year.
2. Geta are a type of footwear consisting of a wooden base held on by fabric straps, similar to western "thongs" or "flipflops." They may be elevated by one or two so-called "teeth," or wooden blocks.
3. Koma-geta are a style of geta with low teeth.
4. The literal translation of the Japanese term he uses for his "occupation" as a "moral scholar," dōgakusha, is in fact "scholar of the way": that is to say, the (Chinese) way of the Tao, as in Lao Tzu's Tao Te Ching (meaning approximately, "the way of integrity"). The strict sense of the term dōgakusha is "Taoist scholar," which seems inappropriate here. By late Meiji, however, the word may refer

just as well to a Confucian philosopher, or to something more like
"moralist" in general. Moreover, it has taken on a mocking connotation of eccentricity—a scholarly person who is so concerned
with morality and reason that they are in the dark about affairs of
the world.

CHAPTER 4

1. Mushanokōji draws on the work of the Belgian playwright and
   philosopher Maurice Maeterlinck (1862–1949) in formulating a literary philosophy that emphasizes pleasure and self-love.
   Mushanokōji adopted Maeterlinck in place of Tolstoy as an exem-
   plar for his own philosophy, finding him less restrictive than the
   Russian, whom he had formerly idolized (Anna Neima, *The Utopi-
   ans: Six Attempts to Build the Perfect Society* [London: Picador, 2021]).

CHAPTER 5

1. This is, of course, "*Civilization and Education*," the book he purchased
   at Maruzen bookstore at the beginning of the first chapter. It is likely
   to be an early work by Paul Georg Münch (1877–1956), a Leipzig-
   born pedagogue, who wrote on the topic of educational reform as
   early as 1908, though I have not been able to trace it [MG].
2. Jibun's ideas about masturbation are progressive for the time
   and substantiated by Western scientific ideas, such as those of
   the Russian born 1908 Nobel Prize-winning biologist Élie Metchnikoff. In his *Nature of Man*, Metchnikoff describes the practice
   as common to all races, and: "the result of a natural disharmony
   in the human constitution, of a premature development of sexual
   sensation" (Metchnikoff, *Nature of Man: Studies in Optimistic Philosophy* (London: Heinemann, 1903) 96.
3. The subject of their conversation, *dōraku* or libertinism, is a contemporary issue of moral debate that emerged during the Meiji
   westernization. See for example, Jason G. Karlin's "The Gender
   of Nationalism: Competing Masculinities in Meiji Japan," *Journal
   of Japanese Studies*, Vol. 28.1 (Winter, 2002), 41-77.

CHAPTER 6

1. The German Art Nouveau and Symbolist painter, Ludwig von Hofmann (1861–1945).
2. Mushanokōji refers to him as the *shosei*, a dated Meiji/Taishō era term, the literal meaning of which is close to "student" or "calligrapher." It referred to someone whose principal occupation was study. When, in 1872, the first modern education system was established in Japan, students from rural areas started moving to the cities to attend high schools and universities. They were usually poor and lodged in the private residences of local philanthropists, performing housework and miscellaneous chores, or calligraphy, as payment. It was considered a status symbol to be providing board to a *shosei*.
3. Max Klinger (1857–1920); Otto Greiner (1869–1916).

CHAPTER 7

1. The Meiji Restoration instituted the *kazoku* (Magnificent or Exalted Lineage) in 1869, as a measure in its campaign of modernization. The *kazoku* supplanted the earlier feudal system with an aristocracy designed to support the emperor. It was abolished in 1947.
2. A *fundoshi* is a traditional men's undergarment or loincloth.
3. Despite its aim to enhance the status of previous outcastes, the Meiji government's revision of the *koseki* household registration system preserved certain pejorative distinctions. In such a manner, the term *shinheimin* ("new commoner") points out someone who was previously considered as underclass. By signing himself as he does, the uncle accuses the inn of having treated him insultingly. See David Chapman, "Geographies of Self and Other: Mapping Japan through the Koseki," *Asia-Pacific Journal* 9.29 no. 2 (2011).

CHAPTER 9

1. The famous tale of Onatsu and Seijūrō is an instance of an extensive love-suicide genre of narrative from the Edo period and became prominent in later literature, kabuki theatre, and film. See

Michael Brownstein, "Sedge-Hat Madness: A Translation of Chikamatsu Monzaemon's *Onatsu Seijūrō Gojūnenki Uta Nenbutsu*," in *Monumenta Nipponica*, 71.1 (2016).

CHAPTER 10

1. Jibun refers to the *Gakushūin*, a school in Tokyo attended by Mushanokōji, which was established to educate children of nobles.
2. *Jugend* ("Youth") was an avant-garde art magazine published in Munich between 1896 and 1941.
3. Fidus, aka Hugo Reinhold Karl Johann Höppener (1868–1948), was a German artist and illustrator. This drawing appeared in a 1919 issue of *Jugend*.

CHAPTER 11

1. The surprising reference to Tsuru's hair color may refer to a subtle "red" shade or overtone, when her rich black hair is seen in a certain light. There is, furthermore, an apparent symbolic reference to the red "crown" of the Japanese crane (*tsuru*).
2. Manryū was the professional name of a renowned Akasaka red-light district geisha, Shizu Tamukai (1894–1973). Manryū's name means literally "ten thousand dragons" and Tsuru's name, "crane," two extremely auspicious symbols. In Japanese, Jibun's final remark here may be read as a pun, along the lines, "How much more beautiful cranes are than dragons!"

Two People

1. Mushanokōji privately published a collection of essays titled *The Wilderness* (Japanese title, *Arano*) in 1908, two years before writing *The Innocent*.

A Dead Friend

1. In Hauptmann's *The Assumption of Hannele: A Dream Poem* (1892), a neglected, delirious peasant girl experiences being welcomed into heaven (*Dramatic Works of Gerhart Hauptmann, Vol. 4: Symbolic and Legendary Dramas*, London: Martin Secker, 1914).

Made in United States
Orlando, FL
28 May 2025

61625850R10076